THE ASTERISK ANTHOLOGY

THE
ASTERISK
ANTHOLOGY

VOLUME 2

EDITED BY
DAVID T. NEAL & CHRISTINE M. SCOTT

NOSETOUCH PRESS
CHICAGO | PITTSBURGH

The Asterisk Anthology: Volume 2
© 2018 by David T. Neal and Christine M. Scott
All Rights Reserved.

ISBN-13: 978-1-944286-06-4

Published by Nosetouch Press
Chicago, Illinois

www.nosetouchpress.com

Cover & Interior Design by Christine M. Scott
www.clevercrow.com

CONTENTS

PART I: SOUTHERN GOTHIC

1ST PLACE
MIDNIGHT OIL
Matthew Brady 11

2ND PLACE
JOHN WELLINGTON
C.W. Blackwell 35

3RD PLACE
A TIME OF DARKER GODS
Mark Edward Brooks...53

PART II: CURSED THINGS

1ST PLACE
THE RING
Patrick Berry...65

2ND PLACE
MASTERPIECE
Russell Dorn... 89

3RD PLACE
THE LLANO ESTACADO
Mary Fancher 105

PART III: CREATURE FEATURE

1ST PLACE
A CURE FOR NYCTOPHOBIA
Ali Habashi.. 117

2ND PLACE
GUARDIANS
Nuzo Onoh 135

3RD PLACE
GOD'S COUNTRY
Christa Miller 157

BIOGRAPHIES 177

COPYRIGHTS 181

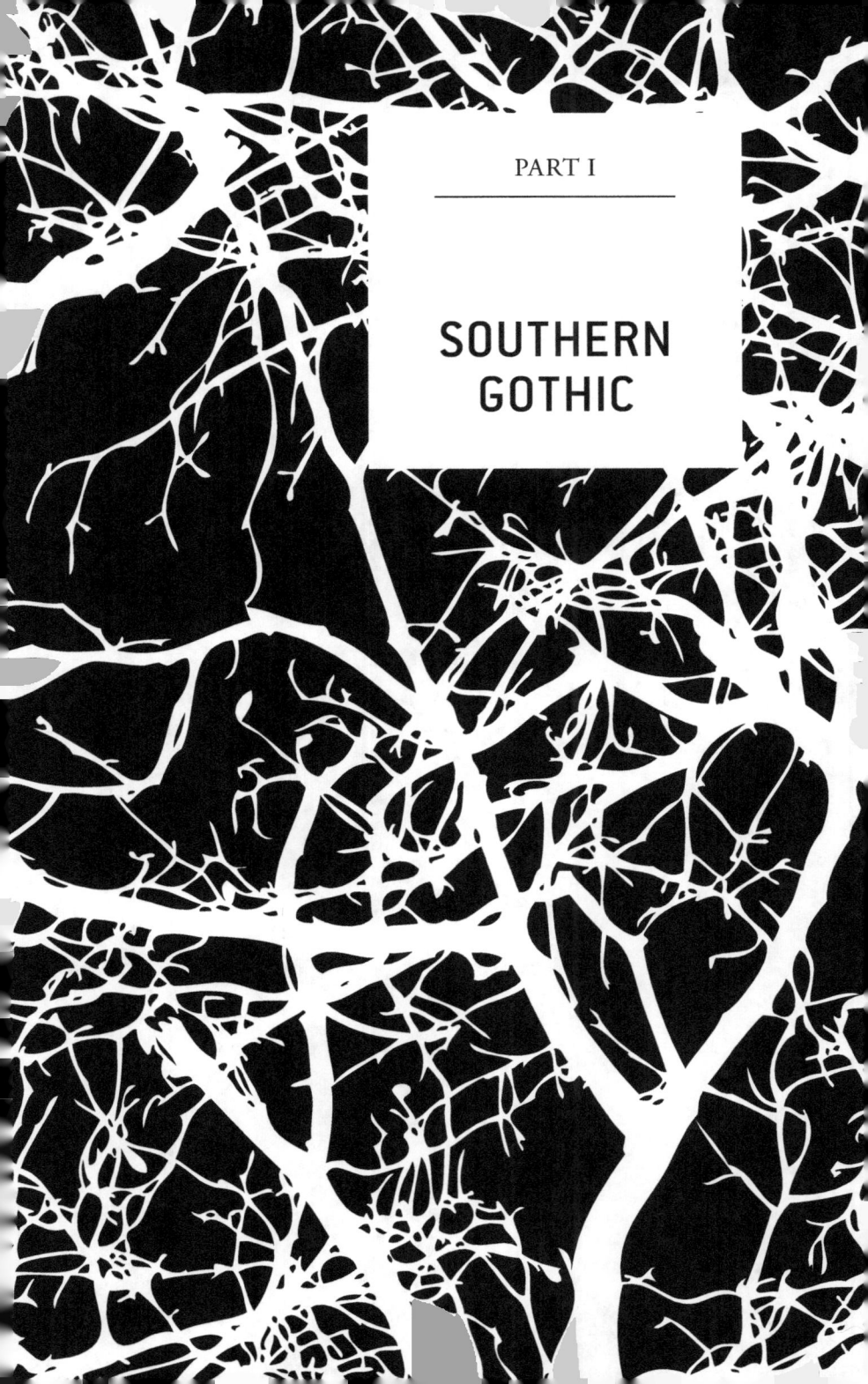

PART I

SOUTHERN
GOTHIC

MIDNIGHT OIL

MATTHEW BRADY

Cole Gunnister had not wanted to live in Midnight Oil since he'd been old enough to know there were other places to be lived in, so it was as much a mystery to him as to anyone who might've asked why he was going back there again.

The town, it had seemed to him then and still seemed to him now, was only an echo of livelier dwellings: the kind of place people stayed at only because they had nowhere else to be. The cramped, lonesome town was sunk squarely in the mouth of a peat bog, right in the humid heart of wetland country, amputated from the greater swath of civilization. No trains or buses ran in its direction. For the traveler without private transportation, the best he or she could hope for in getting there was to hitch a ride aboard one of the turpentine company trucks that ferried mail and other supplies to Midnight Oil six days a week.

Which is exactly what Cole Gunnister did, upon learning of all this to his dismay after stepping off the bus in the next-door town of Bocksten. Sitting in the passenger seat of a truck whose interior reeked of sun-baked leather and gasoline, holding his battered suitcase in his lap, Cole frowned as he scrutinized the folds of his tweed traveling suit. A film of grit and dust was already settling in the creases there, the familiar dirt of his childhood crusting to his fine leather shoes. He'd expected this, of course, but still it did not deaden the sting.

Haven't even gotten there yet and already the place is trying to wear me down, Cole thought as he blew out a breath, elbow propped on the window frame as he surveyed mile after mile of luminous green swamps and creeks.

The truck driver, a craggy-faced man, glanced at his passenger. "So, you said you was from Midnight Oil, that right?"

"I was born there, yes." Cole replied, neutrally.

"Mind if I ask yer name? It's just that I know a lot of the folks there, y'see…"

"Cole."

"Cole…?" the driver prompted.

"Gunnister." Cole grunted.

"Well, I'll be!" the driver hooted. "You're old Judge Gunnister's boy, ain't ya?"

But then his voice sobered, became almost apologetic. He cleared his throat.

"So I'm sure you've heard the news, huh?"

"I have. It's why I'm here."

The driver shook his head, removed his ball cap and scratched his reedy hair. "So how long will ya be stayin', if ya don't mind my askin'?"

His reply was terse. "Just until the funeral. I don't plan on staying an hour longer than that."

"Sounds like this place gets under yer skin, Mr. Gunnister."

"More than you know. And call me Cole."

"Not that it's any of my business, 'course." He coughed, reached behind the steering wheel and flicked on the windshield wipers to scour off the dust and slime of crushed insects on the glass. "Just give yer mother and the others my best wishes, would ya, Cole?"

It was late afternoon when the truck rumbled over the wooden bridge that spanned the brackish creek leading into Midnight Oil. The truck hissed to a stop, and after thanking the driver, gingerly stepping down to the running board, then to the ground, the first thought that struck Cole was that the town was still not much to look at, even after all these years: a changeless, rickety palace of clapboard buildings squatting on either side of one dusty street, a street quietly bustling with mule-drawn wagons and buggies. He could name each establishment, and the proprietors they belonged to, without even having to read the signs: Hogenseth's dry goods store, the barbershop and beauty parlor run by the Osterbys, Miss Amcott's café, a funeral home owned by a one-armed undertaker named Kreepen, and, of course, Tollund's confectionery (the honey of Midnight Oil that drew the children in like flies).

He paused to stare at this last establishment. If he remembered correctly (and he did), Mr. Tollund used to run that shop with his only daughter, Elling, but that was years ago…

The edge of the curtain behind the front shop window twitched, and Cole caught a blurred sight of a face peering out at him intently: a dark, pinched, leathery face with eyes screwed shut. But then a second passed, and it was gone.

Cole blinked, unsure of what to make of what he just saw. He glanced up and down the street, but no one else had seemed to notice. A pair of barefoot young boys, one carrying a hickory switch and the other, a jug of corn whiskey, tipped their straw hats to him as they passed by, while a farmer in dusty coveralls shouldering a hoe cocked his head, observed Cole's clothing and posture, and gaped at the newcomer as though he was a walking scarecrow. From the doorway of his funeral home, Kreepen glowered at Cole with squinted eyes, measuring him from afar.

Cole ignored them, checked the time on his watch, and walked into Tollund's confectionery. The inside of the shop was also just as he recalled it: as cramped and sweet as a sugar cube, its walls and shelves of dark oak a grim contrast to the bright palettes of the jarred candies and pastries. Cole scanned every corner of the shop but there was no sign of the face (or the body it belonged to) that had been watching him from the front window.

He stood there, frowning, before he realized that the young, redheaded woman behind the counter was speaking to him.

"Cole? Is that you?"

"Elling?"

He moved to the counter to speak to her. She was just as pretty as he remembered her to be: the same long, cherry-red hair that flared down to her hips, the same sparkling doe eyes…eyes that watched the world with uncertainty, with suspicion. Eyes that had once poured out so many tears when he stumbled upon her weeping on the steps behind the shop…

Cole felt a twinge in his gut.

"I almost didn't recognize you!" she was saying. "Gosh, you look so different, Collie!"

For the first time since he arrived in Midnight Oil, he smiled. "Not in a bad way, I hope."

"No, not at all! You look…grown up. Professional!"

"My career has been good to me." he said, setting down his suitcase.

"I should hope so. We don't all get to become a fancy lawyer's clerk, you know. Especially if you're from around here."

His smile was mirthless now. "It's because I was from around here that I had to get out."

Sadness came into her eyes. "I'm sorry you feel that way, Collie."

"Oh, don't pay me any mind." he joked, ashamed. "It's just all this traveling, it never did agree with me. Besides, getting to see you again was alone worth the trip."

"Thanks." She beamed at him. "But in all earnestness, you have my condolences for your father. He was a great man." Her eyes clouded with emotion, but with what emotion, Cole couldn't be sure.

"A great man?" he echoed with a frown.

"Oh yes! He did us all proud. And we're all so happy you could be here for his raising…"

"Raising?" he repeated, confused.

"Oh, sorry!" she stammered. "Is that what I said? How silly. I meant his funeral."

"Enough about him." he said, eager to change the topic. Cautiously, gauging her reaction, he inquired, "How about your old man, Elling? Does Mr. Tollund still work here?"

She shook her head slowly. "No. Papa passed away a year ago."

Cole looked down at the floorboards. "Oh…sorry to hear that."

She gazed at him, dreamily, as though he'd said something strange. "Don't be. Papa's still with me."

Cole felt the nape of his neck start to prickle the way it always did when something unnerved him. He decided to hide it, though, so he merely smiled and said, "That's right, Elling. That's right." He scratched the back of his neck. "So...do my folks still live out at the Gunnister Plantation?"

The dreamy look left Elling's face, and her voice regained its normality as she replied, "Sure do. You remember how to get there, right?"

"That's the problem. From here, the place is about a three mile hike through the swamp."

"You could hitch a ride with Old Croghan." Elling offered helpfully.

"Old Croghan?" Cole gaped. "Good god, you mean he's still alive? Wasn't he pushing ninety when we were kids?"

Elling laughed. "He's older than dirt, no arguing that, but he's still kicking. I expect it'd be no trouble for him to give you a lift in his wagon. He's usually parked around The Salt Spring, that little fish-fry down by the river."

"I know the place." he said, quietly, waiting for what she'd say next.

"Hey, doesn't your big brother, Stoney, work there—"

"Yes. He does." he interrupted, straightening the knot of his tie.

"Tell you what," Elling said, turning away, "I'll give the place a call to let them know you're coming." She smiled. "So you don't miss them."

"Appreciate it."

"See you at the big day tomorrow!" she said with unusual cheer before disappearing through the door behind the counter. In the second before it closed, Cole was sure that he saw a shadow of movement. But the door creaked shut, and there was no more to be seen. With nothing more to do, he picked up his suitcase and left, and because of that, he did not hear Elling's muffled voice come floating through the door.

"Can you believe I almost spoiled the surprise, Papa? I'm just getting sillier and sillier, aren't I?" She giggled, and then there was silence before the sound of her voice again. "Of course I like him, Papa, but he can't compare to you. You know that, don't

you? Yes, I'll always be your little girl. He left, but you stayed…
yes, you stayed. You've always been there for me, haven't you,
Papa?" More silence. "I know it. You'll always be here. Always."

––––––––––––––––––

Cole never liked taking any step closer to The Salt Spring
than he had to, but he supposed this was one of those occasions
where he had to. The Salt Spring was a dingy little dancing café
squatting on the muddy riverbank on the edge of town, little
more than a log cabin strung and lit with garlands of colored
light bulbs. The place was much less reputable than Miss Amcott's flowery, tea-scented establishment. Fistfights and public
drunkenness were common. One time, a patron had even been
stabbed to death by a vagrant with a broken liquor bottle. There
was also alligator wrestling on Saturday nights.

Cole walked into the café, not bothering to read the culinary
enticements chalked onto the blackboard that stood by the
door: fried catfish, barbeque, and even alligator tail, plus all the
cold beer you could wash it down with.

Inside, he immediately saw that there were only two people in
the café. One was his older brother, Stoney, who stood behind
the counter in an apron as he dried an empty mug with a rag,
and the other was Old Croghan, who looked even worse than
Cole remembered: ancient beyond ancient, with thin, wrinkled
skin so obsidian-dark and oily as to almost be translucent, and
eyes so sunken and heavily lidded that they looked as though
they were barely open. He wore a pointed sheepskin cap and
wool clothes, but beneath them Cole could still see the naked
curves of his bones bulging through his emaciated flesh.

A faint squelch echoed through the café as Old Croghan
turned his head to look at Cole. Cole, for his part, discreetly
raised a fist to his mouth and feigned a yawn while really trying
to stifle a gag.

Stoney squinted at the new customer before his mouth
stretched into a toothy grin. "Well look who it is, Croggy!" he
boomed in amusement. "Midnight Oil's own prodigal son!"
He threw down the mug and rag, leaped over the counter, and
lumbered over to embrace his little brother. Cole felt the air

squeezed out of his chest, for Stoney was a large man with a boyish, sun-browned face and the build of an ox.

"It's been too long, Stoney." Cole gasped as he patted his brother on his broad back.

"Too long, he says!" Stoney laughed, releasing his quarry but still holding him close as he spun him around to face Old Croghan. "Look here, Croggy! Last time I seen little Collie, he spits in the old man's eye and just marches out of the house, sayin' he's had enough and that he's strikin' out into the world to stake his own claim! Now look at him!" He squeezed Cole's shoulder. "You may be a lot of things, baby brother, but I'd say a liar isn't one of 'em!"

Old Croghan weakly clapped his hands together. They made a wet, splashing sound.

"Can we save this for later, Stoney?" Cole asked. "I'm exhausted."

Stoney blinked, then grinned before he slapped his brother on the back. "Exhausted, he says! Well, all right, little Collie! Elling already called us up on the horn and let us know you needed a ride out to the Plantation! Old Croggy here would be tickled pink to oblige ya! I'd take ya myself, but I'd catch hell from the boss for stepping out on my shift! So away with ya! We'll catch up later!"

Without a word, Old Croghan climbed to his feet from the stool at the counter. His movements were jerky and wooden, reminding Cole of a marionette in an amateur's hands. The old man staggered for the door, squelching all the way in his boots, and Cole was reluctant to follow him outside. The skin on the nape of his neck was prickling.

"Tell the old lady I'll be home as soon as my shift's over!" Stoney cried, playfully punching Cole on the shoulder.

"How's Mom doing, anyway?" Cole asked.

"Busy preparing the fatted calf, that's what!"

"Stoney, I'm serious."

For the first time, Stoney grew somber. "Well, I'm not gonna lie…it hurt her when you left, little Collie. None of us knew what was goin' to happen to ya. We were worried sick…" A strange sheen came over his eyes. "Especially the old man. You wouldn't believe it, but he hardly got a night's sleep after that. You just wouldn't believe it..."

"You're right. I wouldn't."

And with that, Cole wished his brother farewell and left the café.

The ocher cast of afternoon was deepening into a vermilion evening by the time Cole set out for home in the back of Old Croghan's wagon. As grateful as he was for the driver's assistance, there was something in Old Croghan's perpetual silence, squinted gaze, and staccato movements that made Cole content just to sit in the bed of the wagon (strewn as it was with damp straw and cornhusks) rather than join his chauffeur on the seat plank.

With a feeble slap of the reins against the mule's back, the wagon crept forward, rolling away slowly from The Salt Spring café and onto the country road that fed into the darkened maw of what was known to the people in town as Olethe Swamp. Cole looked back over his shoulder at Stoney one last time, who was still waving them off from the café's front porch. He shuddered when his older brother finally disappeared from view and the first of the great pines enclosed around the wagon, for it came to him then that he didn't want to go through the swamp alone (for he did not consider Old Croghan a comforting presence).

But the wagon kept trundling on, its wobbly wheels grounding through the mud and thickets of saw-tooth fern and palmetto fronds. Farther and farther into the swamp they plunged, what little daylight that remained being smothered by the lush canopy of the pine tops where the marsh crows roosted, their throaty cackles almost a taunt to those who passed below. The air was scalding, wet, and thick: to breathe felt like hot oil being laved over one's lungs.

Cole sat miserably in the bed of the wagon, handkerchief over his mouth as he tried to piece together what he could of his surroundings by the emerald motes of the fireflies. By their spectral glow, carpets of moss and pond scum glistened like waterlogged flesh, where dancing dragonflies feasted on whorls of mosquitoes. On hummocks of rubbery grass, Cole spied lounging bullfrogs the size of a man's head, while in deeper waters, more than once he thought he glimpsed a glimmering pair of reptilian eyes skimming just above the surface, only to submerge a moment later before something large cleaved silently through the water.

Cole would have rather encountered whatever was moving under that water than the structure they came upon next.

It was called Lindow's Landing, and it was an indefinable, French Creole dwelling raised right over the deepest waters of Olethe Swamp on tall wooden posts. One had to cross a ramshackle rope bridge suspended over the water just to reach its doorstep. No one in Midnight Oil was sure what the Landing was originally built for, and growing up, Cole had heard all the stories, from the mundane to the outlandish. Some said it had been the home of a simple settler and his family. Others claimed it used to be a chapel or some place of worship. Another faction (a minority, but no less vocal) insisted on something sinister: the Landing had been the lair of an old voodoo queen who bit the heads off bats and chickens to drain their blood before luring in heedless travelers to strip them of their bones, all of which was then mixed and ground together into a paste that she sold as an amulet.

Cole did not give credence to such penny dreadfuls, but even so, looking upon the Landing never gave him a good feeling. With its bousillage walls and dark, hipped roof that flared down over its wide porches, the place spoke of rot and decay and secrecy to him. The fact that the deed to the property had been auctioned off to an unsettling priest of some sort who called himself Doc Lindow (hence the structure's name) did not do much to favorably alter Cole's impression.

Tonight, as the wagon passed by the Landing, Cole could hear the screeching of a fiddle being played from inside the walls. Burning candles were set on every windowsill, while many others placed in mason jars hung from the threading branches of the nearby trees. Cole narrowed his eyes and tried to peer through the panes, but all he could see were hunched shadows tossing against the walls. He could hear the pounding of footsteps on floorboards, and the sound of Doc Lindow singing shrilly, madly, into the night. Cole vaguely guessed that the priest must have been throwing some kind of jamboree.

The wagon passed the Landing, but before the darkness of the swamp could swallow it, Cole saw the plank of wood that was nailed to the lintel above the front door. There was a message scrawled there in black paint that shined in the candlelight:

"Wash me thoroughly from mine iniquity, and cleanse me from my sin."

It was only as the wheels of the wagon began to jolt and the clopping of the mule's hoofs magnified as they struck upon a cobblestoned path that Cole realized he'd fallen into a light doze. Rousing himself, he turned where he sat and saw the spiked iron fences that marked the boundary of the Gunnister Plantation. And then the house itself: a grand antebellum mansion looming in the darkness beyond the graveled drive like a tall, pale temple, illuminated only by the twin lanterns ensconced on either side of the front door.

The wagon rattled to a stop before the fence, with Old Croghan bowed over on the seat plank at such an uncomfortable angle that someone could have easily thought his back was broken.

Cole climbed out of the wagon, brushed the straw and cornhusks that clung to the bottoms of his pants, and cleared his throat. "Umm...thank you, Mr. Croghan."

Slowly, slothfully, the old driver raised his head (his neck making little wet popping sounds as he did), stared at Cole full in the face with closed eyes, then cracked out a smile. Filthy water gushed out from the corners of his mouth and from between crooked black teeth, soaking his lap, and Cole reflexively stepped away, all pretense of politeness forgotten.

Old Croghan jangled the reins, and with a tired snort, the mule began to lead the wagon back the way it had come. Cole looked on as the night and the swamp washed them away, then turned and pushed open the iron fence. It whined on rusted hinges, and Cole made his way up the drive through the yard, frowning at the dead grass and hedges of dead privet. Up close, as he climbed the steps to the door, he saw that the house was in little better condition: the paint was peeling off the columns and soffits and hung there in parched scrolls, listing at the slightest breeze like paper flowers.

He checked his watch and reached out to ring the doorbell, but stopped. Movement from one of the second story windows above him caught his eye. He glanced up, and it was there he saw a group of the plantation servants watching him. They were holding aside the moth-eaten draperies for a better view of him, but they were not the servants Cole remembered. These people, whoever they were, had skeletal faces like waxen effigies, and though they appeared to be scrutinizing him, they did so with closed eyes…

They curtains fell abruptly across the window, and Cole could see no more. The nape of his neck was prickling more intensely than it ever had before.

I'm mistaken, he thought to himself, feverishly. I have to be. It's a trick of the light, of the glass. No one alive can look like that. He reached out again for the doorbell, hesitated, then swallowed. Don't be silly, man! he scolded himself, then rang the bell.

He was answered by none other than his own mother, who studied him warily from behind the golden globe of a kerosene lantern that she held high. But then recognition lit up her eyes, and she embraced him before guiding him over the threshold, back into his childhood home.

He followed her through the large, dusty foyer, their footsteps echoing off the domino black-and-white floor tiling, and through a doorway into the western wing. There they stepped into the dining hall, a stately room whose plaster ceiling was twice the height of its doors. On a sweeping walnut table polished to a luster and lightened by candelabras was a succulent buffet of food, all served on silver platters and dishes and pots: andouille sausage gumbo, boiled crawfish, shrimp and crabs, blackened redfish with dirty rice, Oysters Rockefeller, and creamy corn maque choux. Cole and his mother seated themselves on opposite sides of the table, facing each other.

Cole knew his mouth should've been watering, but he could not pry the image of Old Croghan (or the faces from the second story window) from his mind.

His mother, Arden, still the frail and thin-boned woman he remembered, regarded him with her small, timid eyes and said, "What's the matter, Collie? I thought you'd fancy some vittles after your trip..."

"Oh, it all looks delicious, Mom. It's just..."

"Just..?" she prompted.

He smiled, weakly. "Could I just have some coffee for now?"

"Certainly. I'll call on Mr. Worsley."

She reached for the handbell tied to a cord around her neck and rang it clearly through the dining hall. A moment later came footsteps, accompanied by the rhythmic tapping of a cane. A young servant, roughly Cole's age, appeared in the hall.

Cole was relieved by the familiar (and human) face.

"You summoned me, Madam Gunnister?" Worsley asked with a bow.

"Yes, Mr. Worsley. My son Cole just arrived, you remember him, don't you, dear? You two always used to play together as children, scampering through the gardens and on the rooftops..."

Worsley smiled but did not look at Cole, for he would not have known where to look. Blindness had taken his eyes when he was still a boy. So instead, he simply spoke fondly to the blackness in front of him. "Mr. Gunnister, I'm relieved to hear you've returned home. We've all missed you terribly."

"It's good to be home." Cole lied, his heart slowly breaking the way it always did whenever he looked upon his old friend. "You've all been in my thoughts."

"Mr. Worsley," Arden resumed, "could you fetch our Collie a pot of our finest coffee?"

He bowed again. "It'd be my pleasure, madam."

He withdrew from the dining hall, leaving Cole and his mother alone with their wandering thoughts before they voiced them.

"So how has Worsley been bearing up?" Cole asked, hoping the guilt couldn't be heard in his voice.

"Remarkably well, given his condition." Arden cheerfully replied. "He's been a powerful comfort ever since your father…" She sniffled.

Cole spied an opening. "So how did he go, Mom? You never said in your letter."

Arden dabbed at her eyes with a velvet napkin. Her voice was thick with resigned despair. "Oh, Collie…he fell from the roof and shattered his skull. It happened late in the afternoon. He was repainting the dentilwork." She sobbed. "I told him it was dangerous, that it was servants' work anyhow, but you know how fierce his pride was…" Her eyes were misty with unshed tears, and her voice stiffened. When she spoke again, it was as though she was speaking to herself. "He was a real man. My one and only. He never shirked a task. He did us all proud."

The shout leaped out of Cole's mouth before he could stop it. "What is wrong with all of you? Are we remembering the same person?"

His mother stared at him with the hurt, startled expression of a struck child, an expression that lanced Cole with such remorse that it only enraged him further.

"Fat Christ!" he snapped, pushing back his chair, standing up to step away from the table. He raked his hand through his hair. "Am I off my nut? Even putting aside what he did to me and Stoney, do you not recall the things he did to you? What about—"

But the soft tinkling of porcelain prized him from his rant as he turned and saw Worsley shuffling into the room, taking small, delicate steps as he bore a tray with a steaming pot, a dish, and a cup. Cole glanced at his mother, whose cheeks were now bright with tears, and gnawed his lip but said no more.

Clearing his throat, Worsley asked, somewhat awkwardly, "Where shall I leave your refreshment, Mr. Gunnister?"

"Just leave it on the table, Worsley. I'll take it up to my room."

"Collie, please," his mother pleaded tearfully, "don't go just yet. Stay and tell me why you said such things!"

Cole was not moved. "What time is the funeral?"

"Collie…" his mother moaned.

He turned to ask Worsley. "Worsley, what time?"

"Dawn, Mr. Gunnister. Five a.m."

"Stop calling me that!" Cole barked. "It's Cole, Worsley! I shouldn't have to tell you that!"

"Very good, Cole." Worsley said, setting the tray on the dining table with a heavy clatter.

Cole's room was on the second floor of the Gunnister Plantation, down a carpeted hall hung with congested oil paintings of scowling forebears in trailing black robes and grey curling wigs: each of them the judge of a previous generation. The last portrait to hang on the wall bore the visage of his father, a stern face of razored iron. Cole tried to ignore these paintings but the childhood paranoia caught up to him again and he imagined the eyes in each painted face following him as he moved down the corridor.

He trotted into his room and swiftly closed the door behind him.

He set his cup of still-steaming coffee on the bureau and tossed his suitcase onto his four-poster bed, which sprayed up a thin breath of dust. He then undressed by the light of the oil lamp in front of the cheval mirror and examined himself. He traced his fingers over the familiar, arrowhead-shaped scar behind his left shoulder, over the scorched patch of broken leathery skin from where his father had pressed the clothes iron all those years ago that felt more like days.

He reached for the coffee, drained it in one long gulp, and then set the alarm clock before dousing the lamp and crawling into bed beneath the sheets.

The voices were muffled but they awoke him all the same. Cole blinked into the darkness of the room, unsure of how long he'd slept, and realized there was a strange, bitter taste on his dry tongue. The sheets were cotton but they might as well have been wool, for he was drenched in sweat. It required far too much effort to move, but still he managed to sit up against the high headboard. The voices were still there, conversing just on the other side of the door, so, very quietly (and very weakly), he eased off the bed and tiptoed over. Crouching by the door, palms pressed against the wood for balance, he put an eye to the keyhole and peered into the hall beyond. He saw at once who the voices belonged to.

It was his mother, Arden, and his brother, Stoney. She was fully dressed in her finest clothes, a bonnet over her dark blond hair as though she was going to leave the house at a moment's notice. Stoney was wearing his best three-piece suit, his muscles swollen against the fabric like a sail full of the wind. He was holding the same kerosene lantern that Arden had greeted her son with at the front door.

Cole could hear their every word.

"It's almost time. You think he's out yet, Ma?"

Arden tugged anxiously at the frills of her bonnet. "How would I know, Stoney?"

"Well, Worsley gave him the drink, didn't he?"

"Yes, but I didn't actually see him drink it. He stormed off in a foul temper."

"Yeah, but you said he took it up here with him, right?"

"Right…"

Cole felt very cold all of a sudden, and it wasn't because of what he'd just learned. His mouth felt drier than ever, his skin was growing clammy, and a budding weakness was spreading through his limbs, especially in his joints. He also realized, with a bolt of icy panic, that his breathing was growing more shallow, his heartbeats more rapid.

His vision began to blur, and that is when he backed away from the door, mind racing: What should I do? What should I do? He tried to stand back up, but this caused his ears to ring, and he yelped with fright as his legs buckled and he tumbled to the floor, flat on his back. He could see bright sequins popping in and out of his eyes…

The door to his room flew open, and then he could see his mother and Stoney standing over him, frowns of concern on their faces as they spoke.

"Why is he out of bed?" Stoney boomed. "Worsley, that careless fool! The stuff should've kicked in sooner than this! I told ya ya should've watched him with the dosage, Ma!"

"Miss Rappendam was in the kitchen with him!" Arden chirped in self-defense. "I'm sure she gave him all the help he needed!"

"Well, it's neither here nor there now." Stoney grunted, rolling up his sleeves. "Here, help me get 'im back onto the bed. Mind his head, Ma."

Working together, they hoisted Cole's limp body back atop the mattress. Cole did not protest, for he could no longer move nor speak. He could only stare in helpless, paralyzed dread as his mother walked over to his suitcase and pulled out his clothes. Stoney looked into his brother's eyes and patted him on the shoulder.

"Aww, try not to be too scared, baby brother!" he said happily. "We're not tryin' to hurt ya. We just need ya still for a little bit so we can get ya ready for your big day! Ya wanna look presentable for the old man's raising, don't ya?"

Those were the last words Cole could grasp before an utter blackness grasped him, as well.

———————

A fiddle was screeching in the darkness. A bow sawed against catgut strings in a dusky, hymnal melody that dredged Cole up into wakefulness. His eyes fluttered, then opened, but he could not make sense of what they were showing him.

He was standing (leaning, really) inside an open pinewood coffin that stood with its back propped against a wall. Someone had dressed him back into his tweed traveling suit. When he tried to move and couldn't, he saw that he was bound fast at the arms, torso, and legs by thick leather straps like those on a gurney. The only thing he could move freely was his head, which he used to fearfully absorb his surroundings.

He was inside what appeared to be a shack, a shabby dwelling with bousillage walls that reeked of wet, rotted wood. His eyes widened. At once, he knew exactly where he was. He was inside Lindow's Landing.

And he was not alone.

Rows of folding chairs had been set out in the center of the floor, divided into two wings by a center aisle that led to a sort of makeshift altar where a closed coffin was laid out on a pair of sawhorses. There were burning bundles of sweet incense and standing sprays of violets, honeysuckle and tiger lilies, but they did little to wrest attention from the coffin itself: greenly waterlogged and robed with pond scum, dripping fresh pools of brackish water onto the floorboards.

Hanging on the wall behind the coffin was the oil portrait of his father, Judge Gunnister. There was the faintest trace of a smirk on the otherwise severe face. Had that always been there? Cole wondered. He could no longer be certain.

Cole looked upon this strange funerary scene with bewilderment, a bewilderment that edged into foreboding when he looked upon the seated attendants.

Their heads were bowed as though in prayer, but he still recognized them. They were the people of Midnight Oil. People he'd grown up with. People he'd known all his life: the Hogenseths, the Osterbys, Miss Amcott, Kreepen, Elling, Worsley, and his own mother and brother. But mixed in disparately among them were grotesque figures more horrifying than even Old Croghan: a congregation of shriveled mummies, many little more than skeletons, with faces like withered apples and waxen flesh tinted to a shade of ink or clay or rust. There was the late Mr. Tollund, sitting by his daughter, and there was the late Miss Rappendam, the former head servant of the Gunnister Plantation, seated by Worsley.

He stared at them all, transfixed with disbelief, and gasped, in spite of himself. Every head, living and dead alike, turned to look at him. Every face smiled, but only one voice sounded through the Landing.

"Bless his heart, the poor boy looks as though he's never seen a bog body before!"

The attendants chuckled warmly as a tall, cadaverous man in a black kimono holding a fiddle in one hand and a palmetto fan in the other sauntered down the aisle toward Cole, who squirmed at his approach, for this was the man known as Doc

Lindow. He cut a ghastly figure. He had bulging eyes but no eyelids, cracked, scaly skin, and a thin curtain of wispy, greasy hair that only grew behind his sallow skull. He wore a black bowler hat on his head, and he had a very wide mouth, which stretched even wider when he spoke to Cole, disclosing rows of blocky teeth mortared in ample, horse-like gums.

"Welcome home, Cole Gunnister! Today is a very special day! There are not one, but two occasions to celebrate!"

"Let me go!" Cole yelled, struggling against the straps. "What is going on?"

"Why, today's the day of your father's raising!" Doc Lindow exclaimed. "Very soon now, the honorable Judge Gunnister will walk among us once again!"

"You're insane." Cole said in a measured tone, trying to stay calm, guarding against the panic he could already feel circling him. "My father's dead. Today is his funeral!"

"You're mistaken, my little beignet." Doc Lindow cooed, putting a gnarled finger under Cole's chin. Cole shuddered. "His funeral was a year ago today, but you don't call, you don't write. We had to tell you something to get you to grace us with your presence, didn't we?"

There was nothing Cole could think of to say.

"But don't you worry!" Doc Lindow continued. "We gave your father the proper Midnight Oil sendoff and submerged his body in the sweet waters of Olethe Swamp. Right behind this house, as a matter of fact."

Cole's eyes darted to the dripping coffin on the altar. He whispered, "So that's..."

Doc Lindow smirked, bent over, and reached for a crowbar that rested beside Cole's coffin. He tested the weight of the tool in his hands and Cole flinched, but Doc Lindow ignored him as he turned around and strolled up the aisle to the altar. He stood beside the soaked coffin and spoke to Stoney and Arden.

"Now, as is the custom, will the kin of the deceased come stand beside me, so that they might be the first living souls our departed sees upon his return?"

Cole, along with everyone else in the Landing, watched as Stoney and Arden walked up to the altar and stood by as Doc

Lindow, with extraordinary strength for a man so thin, prized open the lid of coffin with the crowbar. There was a screech of wood and nails, and then a thunderous clatter as the lid flew off to strike the floor. Stoney and Arden rushed over to the coffin, tensed and expectant, and everyone stood up from their seats for a better view as something gurgled inside the box. There was a hushed moment of consummate silence in the Landing before a pair of muddy, slimy arms slithered out to grab hold of the sides of the coffin. A look of intense relief and adoration broke over Stoney's and Arden's faces as, working together, they lifted the bog body from the coffin…the body of Judge Gunnister.

The breath caught in Cole's throat.

Tenderly, gently, they set him on one of the folding chairs, and the mummified Judge sat there trembling, dressed in dripping rags, head bobbing with the confusion of someone who's been pinched awake in the dead of night. The Landing echoed with applause as Doc Lindow took off his hat, bowed, and trumpeted, "Death sunders, but ever the swamp rejoins! Is that not so, my brothers and sisters?"

More clapping, and this time a few even whistled in excitement. At the altar, Cole's family wept tears of joy. Stoney threw his arms around his father in a tight embrace, though it soiled his clothes, and Arden pressed her mouth against her husband's sludgy lips in a hungry kiss, ropes of saliva and mud trickling down her chin.

Panic and madness were wringing Cole apart as he struggled once more against his bindings, though still to no avail. When that failed, he shouted, "I said let me go! Now!"

The Landing quieted somewhat. Doc Lindow ambled back over to Cole and said in a voice loud enough so everyone could hear, "Ah yes, this brings us to our next cause of celebration! The submersion—nay, the rebirth—of Midnight Oil's own prodigal son!"

When the impact of his words sunk in, Cole screamed and thrashed with the ferocity of a trapped wild animal. But still, every face in the Landing went on smiling, as though his zealous resistance was little more than a child's tantrum that amused passersby.

"It is no cause for fright, poor boy!" Doc Lindow soothed with a jovial laugh. To the crowd he joked, "He is like the young lamb trembling before the Shepherd's caring hands!" The audience chortled fondly as he spoke again. "Dearest Cole, what you're about to receive is very special, for Olethe Swamp is a very special place…known only to us. Not only does this swamp rejoin the living with the dead, surely our kind's most primal wish, but it also washes away our every sin from our fellow man's every thought, no matter how blackened with sin we may be." He smiled up at the rafters, serenely, and intoned, "Wash me thoroughly from mine iniquity, and cleanse me from my sin…"

The crowd repeated his words, chanting in unison:

Wash me thoroughly from mine iniquity, and cleanse me from my sin…

Wash me thoroughly from mine iniquity, and cleanse me from my sin…

Wash me thoroughly from mine iniquity, and cleanse me from my sin…

"Cleanse?" Cole bellowed, the last dam inside him breaking now as he swung his gaze frantically about the room, from face to face. "There's no cleansing what's been done in this place!" He looked at Elling. "Elling, how many times did I find you weeping behind the shop, from all those nights when your father put his hands all over you! Can that be cleansed?" He looked at Worsley. "Worsley, what about when we were children and Miss Rappendam beat you when you were late in serving the tea to those nobles? The beating that left you blind? Can that be cleansed?" He shook so hard against the leather straps that the coffin shook. He gazed at his brother and mother. "And Stoney! Mother! Have you two gone insane? How can either of you stand to be in the same room with that man! How many times did he strike us, Stoney, at the smallest provocation? How many times did he torment you, mother? Always threatening, conniving, stealing from you?" Hot, dazzling tears were pricking the corners of his eyes. "And the one time I tried to stop him, what was my reward? A hot iron laid against my shoulder! Do you think someone just forgets that…?" Snarling, he shrieked his refrain, "There's no cleansing what's been done in this place!"

The tempest of his fury spent, he stood there panting for breath, waiting for a reaction. But none came. Everyone was staring at him as though he was merely a lunatic being observed in an asylum. Worsley coughed, Elling clasped her father's hand and stared at Cole with a frightened doe's eyes, while Stoney scratched his head and Arden shrugged hopelessly with mild embarrassment.

"He's been saying things like this since he returned home last night." she explained worriedly. "I'm afeared my poor Collie's suffering a mental breakdown…"

But Doc Lindow began to laugh, and soon his laughter infected everyone else until the whole Landing swelled with it.

"Bless his heart, what an imagination this poor boy has!" Doc Lindow crowed, fanning himself with the palmetto. He smiled at the attendants, but then looked at Cole with humorless bulging eyes as hard and icy as twin hailstones. His voice was a low rumble as he muttered to Cole, "Did I not make myself clear before, dearest Cole? Every sin has been washed away. Death has annulled them. Did you not know? There is no greater forgiveness than death." He leaned in close to Cole, so close their faces were almost touching. The man's breath was the same fetid odor of the swamp. To Cole, it smelled of rot, decay, and secrecy. Doc Lindow said, "You, too, will be forgiven. Is there a greater peace than that? All the pain, all the grief, you caused your family when you left us, that too shall be forgiven…and forgotten."

With those words, every drop of strength evaporated from Cole's body. He did not scream or cry out again even once. Even as the joyous crowd surged forth and lowered him and his coffin onto the floor and nailed down the lid, shrouding him in suffocating darkness. And even as they hoisted the coffin from the ground and carried him out of the Landing onto the wide porches, where a wooden crane waited by the water's edge to submerge Cole Gunnister into Olethe Swamp's forgetful depths.

The turpentine company truck driver who had ferried Cole Gunnister into Midnight Oil was a more sensitive man than he allowed others to perceive. So when the news spread of Cole's disappearance, when the questions were asked and searches were made by the authorities and no fruit was bore of it, he was bothered. He didn't like to think that something dire could've befallen a man he'd looked in the eye and shaken hands with. It left a bad taste in his mouth.

So, more than a year after the news spread, the truck driver paid Midnight Oil a visit on one of his rare days off.

He walked down the one dusty street. He stopped by each establishment and chatted with the proprietors. He smiled and winked and laughed and joked and laced the conversations with the questions he had about Cole Gunnister. But no one had anything important or helpful to tell him. So, when it was suggested by a pretty redheaded woman named Elling that he go and pay a visit to Cole's brother at The Salt Spring café, he was all too happy to oblige, eager for at least one solid lead on this missing man.

The driver walked into the café and sat at the bar, where he spoke with a large man with a boyish, sun-browned face and the build of an ox. He introduced himself as Stoney Gunnister, and after gulping down a couple of beers, the driver steered the conversation toward Cole.

"It's a shame what happened to yer brother." said the driver, wiping a mustache of beer foam from his upper lip. "Seemed like a nice fella. Head screwed on just right, ya know."

"Yeah, bud, it is a shame." replied Stoney, cleaning the empty mugs with a rag. "He was a swell guy. Couldn't ask for a better little brother. Did us all proud."

"Must be rough." the driver added solemnly.

Stoney shrugged and stopped cleaning the mugs. He gazed straight ahead, dreamily. "Could be worse, though. He'll always be with us."

The driver nodded, touched by the sentiment. "Ain't that the truth, fella. Ain't that the truth. Tell me, though, how's yer mother bearing up through all this?"

"Better than most would." Stoney said, proudly. "She's made of iron, and that's no lie."

"Would ya mind if I paid her a visit? To give her my condolences and all that?"

"Sure, bud, no problem. Just let me go fetch Old Croghan real quick. He'll get you to the plantation right as rain!"

The driver was very put off by Old Croghan's appearance, but being a sensitive man, he did not let it show for fear of hurting the old man's feelings. Soon he was sitting beside Old Croghan on the wagon's seat plank as they trundled through Olethe Swamp. The driver spoke on and on about whatever crossed his mind (ball games, politics, the weather), while Old Croghan spoke no words at all.

At length, they came upon Lindow's Landing, where the sound of a fiddle could be heard being played from inside the walls. From the wagon, the driver glanced inside one of the Landing's windows and saw a troupe of hunched shapes dancing in a ring with interlocked arms, the man with the fiddle standing inside the circle, singing out shrilly, madly.

The driver whistled in admiration. He elbowed Old Croghan in the ribs and said, "Hoo-boy! Sounds like they're havin' themselves a gay old time, ain't they?"

They passed on by the Landing, and had the turpentine company truck driver looked a little closer through the window, he would've seen that these shapes were not living, breathing souls but withered husks, and that one of these dancing husks was dressed in a familiar tweed traveling suit.

JOHN WELLINGTON

C.W. BLACKWELL

State of Arkansas, 1848

On the third night, Jessa Olson decided that she would die.

The sky was moonless and beset by unending meteors. Bats tumbled at insects in the clearing above the road. She watched the Dipper wheel through the pines, and she knew that when it reached the eastern grove, the sky would brighten and there would again be the calamity of flies and death birds and the terrifying stillness of human forms all around her.

A dead mule pinned her legs to the road. It loomed in the darkness, a ballast of dead gasses and carrion.

She closed her eyes and counted backward from twenty, the conclusion of which she determined would rend her soul from her body and reunite her at last with her kin. She imagined all the faces she would see from oldest to youngest and then she lost her count and drifted to sleep.

She awoke to a figure leaning over her, shielding the daylight from her face. The head eclipsed the sun in a halo of white sunlight.

"That you, Lord?" said Jessa. It was the first thing she had said in three days, and her words were little more than a whisper.

The figure knelt in the dirt beside her and pressed a cold rag to the girl's forehead. It was a male likeness, larger than she had ever seen.

"I am nobody's lord," said the man. He gestured to the carnage that surrounded them. "But if such a being existed, I would judge him to be at least three days late." His voice was deep and he spoke slowly. He had an accent that Jessa did not recognize.

Jessa found the wet rag with her hands and began wringing the water into her mouth.

The man was now circling the dead mule and touching it with his fingertips. His lips moved silently as if he knew some way to speak to beasts in such a state. His strides were long and deliberate and it occurred to Jessa that maybe he wasn't a man or god but some ancient spirit of the wood.

The man took up the dead mule by the withers and spun it stiffly off the girl's legs and into a rut in the shoulder of the road.

"Can you stand?" said the man. He wiped his hands together. The sun was at an angle to his face and she could now determine his likeness. Jessa's breath stopped in her chest and she covered her eyes with her fingertips.

"I already committed to dyin'," she said. Her voice cracked when she spoke. "So if yer gonna kill me jus' get on with it."

"I'm not going to kill you."

Jessa sat up and slid her hands down her cheek.

The man watched her with bleary yellow eyes.

"What kinda person are yeh?" said Jessa.

There was a faint smile on his face.

"Are yeh smilin'?" Jessa shielded her eyes and squinted. "I cain't tell. Wasn't meant to be funny."

"You addressed me as a person." The smile was there again, his blackish lips drawing back slightly at the corners. "It's a good beginning."

"Well. Figured maybe yeh was in a fire."

"No," he said. He untied a deerskin from his belt and handed it to her. "The fires of creation, perhaps."

Jessa drank, watching the man over her nose. She wiped her mouth corners and blinked.

"What do they call yeh, mister?"

"I go by John Wellington," he said.

Jessa hobbled among the dead, stooping to touch each of the fallen and say their name aloud. Her mother lay sprawled in the center of the road, a dark wound running along her neck like a chinstrap. She found her father across the road, strung from a cottonwood tree and stabbed in both legs. A stain darkened the road beneath him and trailed off toward a stream in the distance. She did not weep until she found the boy. Just a small and fragile form with a toy soldier burrowed beneath his arms as if it were some secret relic of the dead.

John Wellington was kneeling in the road, his sallow face angled at the dirt and his black hair falling all around.

Jessa caught her breath. Flies buzzing in ecstasy.

"John," she said. She looked at him very intently. "Tell me if them robbers is comin' back again."

He shook his head.

"I think they've done their worst," he said.

"They never kilt me." She collapsed in a fit of tears. "How come they couldn't'a kilt me with 'em all?"

John Wellington shook his head again and opened his mouth to speak but he offered not a single word.

———————

By noon, they had built three pyramids constructed of riverstones in the meadow among swatches of larkspur and spider lily. The smell of rot still hung in the road and insects careened haphazardly as if death had merely been a rumor. Jessa took a final look at the cairns as a pair of crows screamed from the branches of the cottonwood tree.

They moved on. They were silent for a long while. The road was not well-traveled and there were many times they had to trudge through muddy streams that carved through the loam with springmelt. The larkspur grew heavy along the shoulders of the road and it reminded Jessa of white clouds in a clear blue sky.

"Where's your family then?" said Jessa. Her knees were beginning to ache as they began a slight uphill grade.

He didn't reply. He had found a long branch and was using it to choose his steps and knock stones from the path.

"You headed to Tennessee?" she said, as if the first question were no longer pending.

John stopped and squinted at the horizon. He drank from his deerskin.

"Choose a question," he said. "But I will only answer one."

"You keepin' secrets, John?"

"Is that your question?"

She gave him a hard look.

"Alright, let me think on it."

They walked a bit farther and then she stopped and folded her arms. She poked at the canvas satchel he carried over his shoulder.

"I want to know about yer ma and pa."

John Wellington leaned on his staff and closed his eyes as if listening to something far off and lovely.

"You want to know about my parents," he said.

"That's what I said."

John Wellington shrugged. "It's too bad. I was going to tell you where all the gold was buried."

She scowled and clicked her tongue at him.

He was smiling again. That strange, burly grimace like something carved in wood.

"My father was a scientist. Brilliant, but not without his troubles."

"Scientist? Cain't say I heard of it," said Jessa.

"Someone who discovers things. Tests new ideas."

"Like Benjamin Franklin maybe."

"My father knew of his work."

"And what about yer ma?"

John Wellington scratched at a veiny patch of skin on his shoulder. He slowed and tapped his staff in the dirt.

"I never had one."

"Everybody's got one whether they knows it or not."

"I was perhaps in many different wombs at different times. Like siblings, older and younger and of different races. Stitched together as one. An orphan and an orphanage all at once."

Jessa was listening but she remained silent, trying to make sense of it. The light was beginning to change. A faint glimmer in the crowns of the maple trees.

"What'd they call him, yer pa?"

"His name was Victor."

"There's a preacher down in Shreveport goes by that name. Think they know each other?" said Jessa.

"No, they do not know each other."

"How can yeh be so certain? Anyway, would yeh like hearin' bout my ma and pa?"

"Yes, I would."

———————————

By evening, Jessa could walk no more.

John Wellington scouted for a campsite and found a clearing beside a gnarled oak tree that brambled at the sky, stock-still and grey as granite. There was a slope beyond the tree and a stream could be heard burbling across the field. He was constantly stooping and passing his hands along the grasses to collect things from the ground and tuck them into his canvas bag. By dusk, he had built a fire from the branches of a dead sycamore. In the center of the fire, he arranged a small shelf made of flagstone and he watched as it smoked off the dust and dirt. A spider skittered crazily over the stone then rappelled to its doom.

Jessa watched him tend the coals. When the fire cooled, he fetched a handful of plants from his bag and arranged them on the flagstone. Black morels and crow garlic. They whispered on the stone as if they had secrets to tell. After a while, he covered these with fresh sorrel and when the sorrel began to wilt he flicked it all into a wooden bowl with a pair of small sticks and handed the bowl to Jessa.

"Thank yeh, John. I never et nothin' like it but it smells wonderful."

"Eat what you can," said John. "In the morning, we'll try to reach Little Rock. Might be a day's walk and then some."

"Is that where you're headed, then? Little Rock?"

"No. I have business farther north."

He was now looking over a letter he had removed from the satchel and holding it to the light.

"Never struck me as a businessman, anyhow," said Jessa.

"Not that kind of business. I've had a correspondence with a man in Brooklyn."

She put the bowl to her nose and inhaled.

"Well. I thank yeh again."

He looked at her strangely, then squinted at the treeline. His yellow eyes glimmered in the firelight.

Something wasn't right.

"Behind the tree," he said.

Jessa's mouth was full of food.

"What now?" she muttered.

"The tree." He wagged his finger at the oak. "Hide."

There was a rifleshot and John Wellington toppled into the fire. Blood hissed in the embers. He righted himself and touched his shoulder tenderly, shirt smoking.

Jessa screamed. There was another shot and the rifleball whined somewhere in the half dark twilight. John Wellington scooped the girl in his arms and barreled toward the oak tree. He smelled like blood and woodsmoke.

"Can you climb?" he said. His voice was a grim whisper.

Jessa was frozen with fear.

John Wellington lifted her to the first branch and pointed to the next highest bough.

There was shouting in the field. As Jessa climbed, she could see two men lumbering toward the campfire, one with a long rifle and the other with some kind of wood axe held aloft. When the man with the axe passed near the fire, Jenna began to cry.

"You no good bastard," she yelled.

The men searched the darkness for the voice.

"Where you at, young miss?" called the man. He was squinting at the tree as if he had surmised her form in the branches.

"I seen you. Yer the one kilt my kin," she cried. "Go to hell."

The two men were now standing under the tree, looking up. The girl crouched in the branches like some wayward bird blown off-course and stranded.

"No need for that. Now where'd that big ugly devil run off to?" said the man. "We wanna have talk with him."

Jessa was spitting and breaking off twigs to throw at them.

The men looked around.

"Now why don't yeh scurry down from there, darlin'. Consider yourself rescued."

"I ain't comin down never," she said.

They looked at each other.

"Think yeh can shoot her down off them branches, Sebb?" said the man with the axe.

Sebb nodded.

"Jus' that we ain't got much powder. Done shot up the vast countryside since the day after Easter."

"Well then, yeh declarin' this country is vast, is yeh?"

"Reckon it's vaster than most." Sebb spat on the ground and wiped his mouth with the back of his hand.

"Shoot her, dummy."

Sebb raised the rifle and tapped a few grains of powder into the pan. He pulled the cock and lifted the rifle to his shoulder.

There was a sound in the darkness, like an animal groaning. Something dark passed beneath the branches and struck Sebb in the forehead with a ruinous crack. He crumpled and fell with the rifle at his feet, legs spasming in the dark grass. A wet riverstone cambered end over end and settled on an exposed root at the base of the oak tree.

John Wellington appeared at the fringes of the firelight. There was another stone in his hand and he was shouldering slowly toward the man with the axe, his eyes fixed and narrow.

The two men did not exchange a single word.

The man raised his axe above him and planted his feet in the dirt. His eyes darted at the rifle on the ground as if judging whether he could reach it. John Wellington quickened his pace, and as he closed the distance, he launched the skull-sized stone. It struck the man in the center of his chest and sent him reeling backward. The axe fell to the ground and John Wellington quickly recovered it. He stood over the man with the axe held at his side and the iron bevel shining in the fireglow. He spun the thing in his hand as if he had been doing so his entire life. He paused and turned to Jessa. It took him awhile to find her silhouette in the darkness.

"Kill him, John," she said. "Do it for my Ma and Pa. For Willy, too."

The man was heaving on his side, still unable to find his breath.

John Wellington slipped the axe handle in the waist of his trousers and lifted the man by his ankles like a wheelbarrow. He dragged him past the tree and down the slope to the center of the stream. He crouched over him as if performing some religious incantation. There was a momentary thrashing in the black water. A pair of pheasants launched from the cattails and faded to the sky like bats.

When he returned, he was alone. He rubbed his face with his hands and stared about the field.

"Are you hurt, John?" Jessa called.

He tapped his shoulder with the tips of his fingers but didn't say whether he was or wasn't.

"Are you still hungry?" he finally said.

Jessa put a hand on her stomach and admitted that she was.

When she awoke, the sun had not yet risen and there was a thin rind of mist that clung to the fieldgrass. The fire had fallen to a white ash. She thought for a moment that John had left her while she slept, but she found him standing in the stream dressing his wounded shoulder with cattail leaves. He saw her coming and pointed to a jumble of rocks on the slope of the streambed. There were three passionflower fruits grouped together like eggs in a nest. He pinched his fingers together and put them to his lips in a pantomime.

She looked at the fruit and then looked away.

"John," she said. "You said *orphan* before. Is that what I am now?"

"Yes," he said. "But in that way we are siblings."

"What will I do when we get to Little Rock?"

"You will find a magistrate. He will know what to do."

"I don't even know what that is. I cain't come to Booklin' with yeh?"

"*Brooklyn.* No, you cannot."

"Why not?"

"It's better I travel alone."

"But why?"

He looked at her and then looked to the road as if he had heard a sound. Jessa shrunk into the streambed and peered in the direction he was looking.

"What do you hear, John?"

He stood frozen for a moment, then pulled the woodaxe from a loop he had made in his waistband.

"Come with me," he said.

———————————

There was a mule cart in the road with no mule or horse to be seen, and in the cart was a man chained by his wrists to each railing like some abandoned Christ. He heard them coming up the road and raised his head, a bloody mess of swollen lips and eyes.

"Y'all friendly now?" called the man.

Jessa looked at John Wellington.

"We ain't them robbers if that's what you mean," she said.

The man rattled his chains against the cart.

"Lord them robbers. Killers." He coughed and spat blood and saliva over his chin. "Ain't enough curses to tell what they all done."

"John kilt 'em both dead," said Jessa.

The man seemed to nod.

"I know. There's another man they's with. Calls himself Duncan. He saw it all. He took the mule thataway last night. Left me to die."

"Hold still and I'll get you free." said John Wellington.

"Free?" said the man. "Ain't no freedom down this way."

"How'd yeh end up with them anyhow?" Jessa said.

"Caught me on the road," said the man. "Thought I was a runaway. Showed 'em my papers and they jus' tore 'em up. Said they'd take me to a judge for a bounty even though ain't no bounty to be had. Glad you kilt all you did."

John Wellington smashed the chain with a slab of granite he had found in the road and the man's arm fell by his side.

"What is your name, friend?" said John.

"They call me Soules."

"You headed north?"

"All the way to Canada if I can make it. Got a sister in By-town. Best baker ever done lived. Reckon I jus' follow the smell all the way."

They helped Soules from the wagon and when he got to his feet he just stood there in the road. Wet blisters on his wrists from the iron chains. He teetered in a circle and squinted at the sky. John Wellington took his hand and held it.

"Follow along until your eyes heal," said John.

They walked together as the day became bright and birds flooded the trees with a great bewailing of sounds. The trio looked like some parable that had not yet been sorted out and whose lesson was still unclear.

When the temperature rose, they stopped at a spring to drink and refill the deerskin. Turtles slipped nervously into the water as they neared and dragonflies pitched and hovered in the air.

"Your arm," said Soules. He was blinking and wiping water from his mouthcorners.

John Wellington glanced at his own arm as if he might see something unexpected there.

"What about it?"

Soules squinted and rubbed his eyes again.

"Looks like my skin is all."

"I would agree that it does," said John Wellington.

"But the other one," Soules couldn't finish the thought out loud.

"It is not the same."

Soules was still squinting and looking up and down as if trying to make sense of what he had said.

"Duncan said there was a monster in the field. That's what kilt them old boys and that's why he got scared and run off. He wasn't right about it was he, John?"

John Wellington didn't respond. He drank from the spring and cooled his head with the water.

"John ain't no monster," said Jessa. "He jus' an orphan like me."

"Don't mean nothin' by it."

"Go an' look at your own self in the pool," she said. "Nary a Prince Charmin' among yeh."

Soules shook his head. "Said I didn't mean nothin'."

Jessa was now standing in the road, looking out at the hills on the horizon. Her arms were crossed and her nose twitched like a rabbit.

"Yeh smell that?" she said.

"My sister's sweetbreads," said Soules. "Told yeh to follow the smell."

Jessa was pointing. "Ain't no sweetbreads," she said. "There's smoke thataways."

On the hillside was a column of woodsmoke that funneled upward and flattened along the ridge like a thunderhead. There was a clearing where the smoke was rising and small structures dotted the space around it.

They drank some more and watched the smoke change directions with the Ozark wind. It wasn't long before a mule cart appeared on the road just a few miles away. It moved like a toy pulled along a string.

"If there's a wagon comin' I don't want to be seen," said Soules.

"I don't believe there's trouble," said John Wellington. He was watching it intently. "But it's better to be safe." He motioned to Soules and climbed a stony embankment toward a thick line of bushes above the road.

"What about me?" Jessa said.

"Better you stay in the road," he said. "If they're friendly you can ride to the next town."

"And if they ain't friendly?"

"Likely they're friendly enough."

"But you was takin' me to Little Rock," she said.

"I was takin' you to the law to get sorted out," said John Wellington. "You belong with a family."

"I thought I had a family."

John Wellington stood beside her. He looked as if he were a hundred times her size. He took her hand.

"You cannot stay with me," he said. "When the cart stops, tell them what happened. We'll be watching."

Jessa folded her arms and stomped in the dirt.

The two men disappeared behind the brambles on the hillside and soon Jessa was alone on the road. She stood like a wooden carving of a child, still and stone quiet. Only the eyes moved. There were crows in the field picking at the earth and staring at her with tilted gestures. She watched them.

Soon she could hear the clomping of hooves on the road and the mule cart appeared with a single mule and a grey-haired couple sitting up in the cart. They didn't see the girl until they were nearly on top of her and then they pulled the reins. The old woman held the reins and the old man was slumped beside her with bandages on his neck and arms.

"That a youngern I see in the road?" the old lady called. She had a black patch over her eye and her right ear was just a small nodule of mottled skin like the inside of a cat's ear. It had either been burned or cut away.

Jessa didn't respond. She just looked at the ground sadly.

The old man was badly burned and the bandages were wet with sweat and blood. He covered his head and did not speak.

"If you're lookin' for a ride, get in. But Reggie needs lookin' after," said the old woman. "We had a barnfire and now we huntin' a doctor."

Jessa looked at the hillside and then at the old couple.

"My family was robbed," she said.

"What now?" The old woman cupped her hand over the fleshy florette where her ear had been.

"Robbed," said Jessa. "Jus' a couple days' walk from here."

"Well climb in but don't be slow 'bout it," said the old woman. "I told yeh we got to hurry."

There was a sound from the hillside. The bushes shook. The old woman took the reins in her hands and rested a shotgun on the edge of the mule cart. She looked in the direction of the sound then back to Jessa.

"Darlin' you best get in or get left behind."

Soules appeared in the brushline, flailing his arms and slapping his body all over. There were insects zig-zagging the air around him in a cloud. He let out a desperate cry and tumbled down the slope, squirming and flailing with a litany of curse words and invectives such that Jessa had never heard in her life.

The mule stomped in the dirt and shifted to its haunches as if it were about to rear. The old woman juggled between the shotgun and the reins.

"Ambush," yelled the old man.

Soules toppled into the road in such a frenzy that he appeared to be consumed by some invisible fire. The air was alive with the sounds of tiny wings.

For a moment, the woman looked as if she had gained control of the shotgun, but as she leveled it over the mule cart, John Wellington appeared beside her and lifted the weapon from her hands. With his free hand, he touched the mule's neck and began to speak to it in a foreign tongue. The mule stepped and snorted and then was still.

When the old woman got a good look at John Wellington she leaned into Reggie and covered her mouth with her hands. The man held her for a moment then lifted a Bible into the air.

"In the name of Christ let us pass, Devil," he yelled. He swung the Bible at a wasp as it hovered before him.

The woman grabbed the reins and snapped them against the mule's hide but the mule only shifted slightly where it stood.

"The Devil put a spell on it, Reggie," cried the woman.

John dangled the shotgun in the space between them.

"I'm going to leave this in the road and you can come back for it if you please," he said. "In the meantime I bid you a safe journey." He stroked the mule's withers and spoke to it again and the animal began to walk in a slow trot.

The man stood in the mule cart with the Bible still in his hands as they advanced down the road.

"Return to hell, Demon," he shouted. "You burned our barn and we'll watch you burn, too."

John Wellington waved politely. Jessa was still standing in the road pouting and Soules was halfway across the field swatting at insects. John cinched the canvas satchel around his neck and continued down the road.

They reached the farm within an hour. The barn lay in a collapsed heap of charcoal and iron and a furious black smoke welled from its crackling heart.

"Why'd they say it was you, John?" Jessa was holding her palms toward the conflagration as if judging the temperature.

"They don't know who did this," he replied. "But it's the unknown they fear the most."

"It was Duncan," said Soules. He was leaning against a fruit tree rubbing at the welts on his arms. "Bet he started the fire so he could rob the farmhouse. Maybe he's still close by."

John Wellington gazed about the property. The farmhouse was just a small pinewood structure with a two-horse stable behind it. The front door swung and creaked in the breeze. A dead dog lay in the dirt not far from the swinging door.

"We ain't gonna stay here, are we, John?" Jessa said.

John Wellington looked at the dog then back to the creaking door. He had much the same expression of worry as the night he killed Sebb and the other man. He shook his head.

They took a trail off the main road that wound through hills of knee-high sedge and phlox that spilled through the oakshadows like pink hallucinations. They could sense the river long before it came into view, an unseen power that drew them as if by some magnetic property.

When they finally reached the southern bank of the Arkansas River, Soules waded up to his waist and coated his skin with river silt. John Wellington trudged along the riverbed to a place where the water had excavated the roots of a hickory tree.

He crouched in the dark water for a few minutes, and when he returned he held in his hands an ancient-looking catfish. It lay still in his arms save for the pumping gills, as if it had somehow been tamed.

They built a fire from piles of driftwood and cooked the catfish on a long riverstone laid through the center of the fire.

"Little Rock is not far," said John Wellington. He was looking at Jessa when he said it. She was pulling meat from the ribs of the catfish and looked up. "We'll reach it by mid-morning."

"What about Soules?" said Jessa.

"I'll stay with John," said Soules. His body was entirely mud-cracked with silt. "Till New York, that is."

"Y'all cain't wait to be rid of me, cain't yeh?" There were tears in her eyes glittering in the fireglow.

"You're the same danger to us as we are to you," said Soules. He loosened a piece of flesh from the catfish and held it in his hand. "Look like we done took you. That's what folks'll think."

"You're tough," said John Wellington, "But this country is tougher on folks like us, Soules and I. You'll know about it soon, if you don't already."

John straightened suddenly and held out a hand in a gesture of silence. The others froze and listened. There was only the great coursing of water and the clinking of burning driftwood.

"How many?" said Soules.

"Just one."

"We got time to run?"

It was too late.

A shadow passed over the riverbank and a man appeared before them. He had a long and hairless face and ghastly scar at his hairline as if he had been partially scalped. There was a revolver in his hand and he was grinning wide enough that his rotten teeth caught the light from the fire.

The seated men rose slowly to their feet.

"Hidy there," said the man.

Jessa threw a handful of fish meat at the man.

"I seen you. You was with them men that robbed us on the road."

"You're lucky if that gun is loaded, Duncan," said Soules. "Cause if it ain't, I'm gonna finish what them Choctaw started."

"No way to talk to your old friend," he said. He looked at John Wellington and whistled. "Boy ain't you ugly. They callin' you the Ozark Demon, did yeh hear? Causin' mayhem ever which way yeh go. Killin' folk and burnin' barns."

"You're the demon," said Jessa. She spat at his feet.

"On the contrary," he said. He laughed to himself then fired a round in the air. The muzzle flash brightened his face for a moment. "I'm the hero. I'm the fella done save the little girl from the Ozark Demon and his little runaway."

A dog barked somewhere beyond the riverbank. Then another. The trees flickered with the glow of torchlight.

"You're going to shoot me once," said John Wellington.

Duncan shook his head.

"No I ain't. Bounty's higher if I catch yeh alive."

John Wellington took a step toward the man.

"You're going to shoot me once and then I'm going to drown you in the river." His voice swelled as if powered by the river itself.

He took another step forward.

Duncan stepped back and leveled the revolver.

"I'll do it if yeh make me."

"Then do it, coward."

Jessa covered her face and began to cry.

Duncan thumbed the hammer back.

"Yeh gonna make me, ain't yeh?"

"It's going to happen as I told you."

"Well ain't yeh a mighty fine prognosticator."

Duncan fired.

John Wellington shuddered, but he did not fall. When the man cocked the gun again, John Wellington caught his wrist and pulled him close. There was another shot, and a spark danced in the riverstones. The men faced each other in a tense and unnatural embrace, their noses almost touching, then John twisted the man's arm until it separated from the socket.

Duncan's scream pierced the river valley and welled up through the oaks on the hillside. The dogs howled back in an excited frenzy. Torches could now be seen moving between the trees and flowing down the riverbank like fireflies.

The revolver fell beside the campfire.

John Wellington hoisted the man above his head. For a moment, they looked like some sideshow performers rehearsing by moonlight—faces clenched and wild. John Wellington bent slightly, then heaved Duncan into the river. He screamed again as he careened into the water then quickly disappeared in the current.

John Wellington turned to Jessa.

"I need to ask something of you," he said. He spoke quickly and there was a look of panic in his eyes.

"You're bleedin' all over, John," she said. She touched his shirt and looked at her hands. His blood looked black in the light of the fire.

The dogs were close now and they could hear them whining on the riverbank. Torchlight reflecting on the water. Someone was shouting the word *demon* from out in the dark.

John Wellington lifted his canvas bag and set it over Jessa's shoulder.

"When you get to Little Rock, I need you to bring this to the postmaster. There's money for postage inside. And plenty for you to keep. These letters are very important, Jessa."

She was scared, but she clutched the satchel in her hands and nodded.

"I'll do it, John. Where do I send it?"

"Brooklyn, New York." he said. "Fulton Street."

"We're out of time, John," said Soules. He was standing over them watching the mob grow closer. "The river's our only way out now."

"This part is important," said John. "Listen."

"Fulton Street, Brooklyn." She was repeating it over and over.

"Remember this name," he said.

"Okay."

"Walter Whitman."

She repeated the name.

Soules was wading in the river and they could see dogs kicking up sand on the riverbank. John Wellington regarded Jessa and lifted a bloody palm into the air, then he followed Soules into the water.

The dogs splashed behind them, barking and howling as the two figures bobbed along the scallop-edged current toward the lamplights of the city. Someone fired a futile shot into the river and cursed their escape.

Jessa closed her eyes and buried her face in the canvas bag. The dogs whined and shook themselves. They panted noisily and lolled their tongues. The men were standing around and muttering to each other. One of them said something to her but she only clutched the bag tighter against her face.

It smelled like blood and woodsmoke.

A TIME OF DARKER GODS

MARK EDWARD BROOKS

"'Bout that time, boy."

The old man spit as he leaned back in his rocking chair on the porch where he usually stayed fixed most of the day, weather and weak bladder permitting. He lit a smoke for his pipe with a wooden match he freed from his overall pocket. Then, he removed the oxygen tubes from his nose as the scruffy-headed boy and his spotted little dog came bounding out of the screen door, which was barely hanging on its frame. His old, fading eyes found the horizon filled with dark clouds moving in from the west.

"You need t'hurry up about it. Storm blowin' in quick. Git movin'."

"Yes, Sir, Papa. Come on, Skip," said the boy, heading down the creaky steps past the wiry grey cat with no name. It was early spring—the first Sunday—and the first storm of the season was getting ready to hit. It had been a dry, hot summer last year, and that was bad for this town and the farmers. Papa said this year things would be different…at any cost.

The boy sped past the hog pen as fast as his dirty sneakers would carry him, the foul-smelling beasts crying out in joy, and he noticed another one of the hogs had died. The remaining ones were feasting on the fallen that lay there in the mud. *Survival of the fittest,* as his Papa said all too often. The small hog was being ripped in different direction and the boy turned his eyes away from the bloodbath toward the barn, where the pentagram hung above the open doors.

He entered into the musty darkness and the smell of old hay and dung assaulted his senses. He quickly found the rust-covered bucket in the corner under the three horseshoes by the skinny cow whose last two calves died. He headed out without looking back at her painful noises. There would be no milk anytime soon.

"Gotta make things right again, boy." his grandfather said, coughing on the smoke that had been gnawing at his lungs for longer than the boy had been alive. "Better years ahead, for sure. At least the next five if we do this right. But we got t' hurry now. Mornin' is almost done with. Go on in the house and fetch dem supplies I got thar on the table. Be fast, now!"

The boy took notice of his own reflection in the mirror that hung there by the screen door on the porch. Papa said it kept out evil spirits. The boy was almost twelve, but looked small for his age. That was okay. Papa said he was stronger than most boys. That's what good hard work did to a boy—it made him a man. He entered the kitchen, hefted the box off the shaky table where once four plates sat but now only two, and headed back out into the coming storm.

"Set 'er at my feet thar, boy. See what we got." the old man said, leaning down and coughing some more while rummaging through the contents. "Hold that bucket still while I do this. We ain't got much time left."

The boy knelt down with Skip at his side, ever the curious, loving thing, and watched his Papa sort out the mess. "Got us some nice, fine fruit here." the old man said, carefully placing the shiny apples and cranberries that he had gotten from Old Man Darby two towns over in the bucket. On top of that, he placed a bed of walnuts and pecans. "I hope He likes 'em."

Next, the old man's shaking hands took hold of the few good ears of corn that produced this year, which was not much as the boy recalled, and laid them over the fruits and nuts.

"Give me yer hand, boy." the old man said, producing a carving knife. The boy hesitated and the old man locked eyes with him. "Come on, now! No time fer crybabies. Yer damn near a man. Hold 'er out there and let's be done with this foolishness."

"The corn has to have our blood on it?" the boy repeated from what he had heard his grandfather say over the years. "Ain't that right, Papa?"

"Yea, boy, t' mark our failure." the old man said, gently taking the boy's hand and placing the knife in line with his palms, which were tougher than most boys his age. "You got strong hands and pure blood. You can be proud of that. Only hurt fer a few seconds. No cryin' now."

The boy closed his eyes and winced at the sting that came with the swift cut. He opened his eyes to see his own palm red and the blood being squeezed by his grandfather across the corn, turning it a sickly pinkish color. The old man wiped his blade clean with a handkerchief he produced from another pocket then placed it in the boy's hand and squeezed it tight.

"Now run out back and get a chicken. Plump one."

The boy did as he was told, the dog at his side and the wind at his back, and soon came back with a twitching yard bird in his grasp. He crept up the steps where his grandfather sat with the pipe smoke billowing around his dull eyes and he saw a larger knife on the table next to a jug of homemade wine and Papa's mouth harp, which he hadn't played in months.

"That'll do." the old man said, taking the chicken and holding it over the bucket with one hand while grabbing the knife. "Livestock blood."

"Yes, Sir." the boy said, with wide eyes watching the sacrifice unfold. The blood spilled, and then the old man handed the bucket over to the boy, along with a small box of salt.

"You pour a circle on the ground. Do that dance while I say the words."

The boy did as he was told. He felt like an Indian as he danced around there and his Papa chanted some words in a language he did not understand. When it was over he knew the hardest part was coming. The ultimate sacrifice.

"You know what needs doing, boy." the old man pointed out more than he asked.

"The heart of one you love." the boy repeated from what he had heard ever since he could walk and talk.

"That's just how it's done. The very heart of a loved one." the old man said showing some emotion for the first time since the boy came outside. "We all make sacrifices fer what needs fixin'. Your grandma knew that ten years ago." the old man said, casting a glance in the direction where the boy knew she was buried. "Gave 'er life for this town." he choked back the tears. "Has t' be somebody ya love, boy." he repeated, looking down at the boy's dog and the boy let his gaze follow the old man's, to where Skip sat in the dirt, thumping his little spotted tail.

"I know." the boy said, taking the knife from the old man with tears forming in his eyes and called Skip over to where he was on the porch. "We all make sacrifices, Papa."

"That's right, boy." the old man leaned over and tucked a piece of paper in the boy's shirt pocket. "That's the list of others who are giving this year. Reverend Foyer. Sheriff Taylor. Three others ya may not know. You stop by their houses on the way to the creek and pick up what they have. Addresses 'er all written there fer ya. You know what to do by now. You went with me the last time. You remember the way, son?"

"Yes, Sir." the boy said kneeling down to scratch behind Skip's ear.

"Well, then. Time fer that heart, boy."

"I know." the boy said, taking hold of the dog's collar and gripping the knife high above his head. "Sacrifices have to be made."

"I love ya, boy." the old man said, leaning back for his pipe.

"Love you, too, Papa."

The deed was done. The heart lay on top of the other items in the bucket and the boy was on his way to the Reverend Foyers. When he got there, the good Reverend was already in tears, waiting at the front gate of his small home with the large cedar pines and the cross-eyed goat that gave the boy the creeps. He was holding something bloody wrapped in his hands.

"Take this, son." the holy man said, placing the blood-soaked rag in the bucket. "The lying and gossiping tongue of a sinner. He won't miss it. He never used it well."

The boy saw the body of a man by the honeysuckle bushes near the fence. He looked like an older man and even though his face was turned away he could see the crimson stains on his white dress shirt.

"This town will rise from the ashes again, my son." the reverend said, turning away as the boy headed off down Juniper Road.

"Yes, Sir." the boy shot back feeling the weight of the pail getting heavier.

"You best hurry, boy." a deeper voice called, and when he spun about the Reverend was nowhere to be seen. Only the black goat with the crooked eyes stood there at the gate looking after him. The boy swore it broke into a grin. He turned and hurried down the road for his next stop.

Sheriff Ben Taylor was a big man. The boy's grandmother used to say he filled out his uniform well. Today the big man did not look strong to the boy. He was out of uniform, only wearing some sweat pants and a long baggy Astros T-shirt and his face was pale and staring at horizon where the clouds were ever-building. A low boom of thunder shook the morning skies.

"Best hurry, there, son." the Sheriff said dropping his bloody gift into the bucket. "Those are the eyes of a pedophile, boy. You don't need to know what that is right now, other than to say they have seen things they shouldn't have. He was a bad man. He won't be missed none. I hope it helps this town."

"Yes, Sir, Sheriff." the boy said, and watched the giant light up a smoke and turn to somberly wander back into his dark house.

Papa had said he may not know the last three, but the boy recognized the next man almost immediately. It was Henry Sanford, the retired school principal.

"Hello, son." the portly man said, staggering a bit down the stone path from his humble abode to greet the boy. Papa had said after Mister Sanford retired he took to drinking too much, especially after his wife disappeared a few years back.

"'Morning, Mister Sanford." the boy forced the tiniest of grins. Mister Sanford always dressed nice for school, but now he wore faded jeans and a dirty plaid shirt and smelled of sweat and booze as he leaned down over the boy and his blood-filled bucket.

"This is the hand of a child molester." he belched and let a bottle fall from his grasp with a dull thud to the earth below. "He did some naughty things, this one. Got what he deserved." the man said brushing back his unkempt hair and lifting his gaze to the flashes of lightning to the west. "Hurry on, boy. The darkness awaits! All must be made right to the Darker Gods!"

"Ssshhh!" the boy hushed him and scooted away back to the edge of the road. "Please don't do that, Mister Sanford. You will make him angry."

"Why on earth did your grandfather send you, anyway?" the drunken ex-principal asked, stumbling back a few paces. "You're just a damn kid. Just a boy."

"Papa says I'm nearly a man, now."

"Not yet." the drunk said, sighing deep and closing his eyes to the ominous horizon. "But I guess it will happen faster here for you. If you got a brain in that tiny head of yours, you will get the hell out of this town when you get old enough. Yes, Sir, hop in the first thing smoking and never look back."

"Can't do that, Sir. You know that. He can find you anywhere."

"Sure, sure. You can't run and you can't hide." the fat man said, almost singing in mockery and the boy knew better than to stay close. "The Darker God can see inside."

"I have to go now." the boy said, and headed off for the fourth house on the list.

"Yes, you go on now, son. You go and bow down to that evil damn thing that has been doing nothing but killing. You go and tell Him He will pay one day for what happened to my Lucy! Tell him I am not afraid of Him!"

A shot rang out and the boy jumped, nearly spilling his bucket of offerings. He slowly turned to see Mister Abrams, the town produce manager, standing with a hunting rifle on the porch of the only house opposite the drunken principal's. He tipped his hat to the boy and waved him on.

"I will handle this mess, boy. You go on now and do what needs doing."

The boy did not answer, but kept walking, his pace quickened by the thunder. It was not long before he turned up Berkshire

Road. Normally, this would be a beautiful place but the blue bonnets were not there because of the drought, and the field by the school was just scorched grass. The walk seemed to take forever, and finally The Wooden Spoke bar came into view.

There were only a few trucks there today, but as soon as the bartender—Mister Carter—opened the door, the boy could hear the country music and the clicking of pool balls echoing from within the dark confines. He had a stone glare on his face and walked promptly up to the boy, his eyes narrow and cold, and his steps long in stride.

"The liver of a drunkard. Easy enough to find. Hard to give up." he spat out and slammed the bloody rag down into the bucket and turned on his heel, leaving as quickly as he came, without another word, wiping his rough hands on his apron and mumbling to himself all the way back to the door, which he slammed behind him.

The last stop for the boy on this day of death was at the town library. Miss Jenkins, a middle-aged, plain woman—who had never married nor bore children—crept out the door with an umbrella shading her face, even though a drizzle had not yet begun. She studied the boy carefully over her horn-rimmed glasses and her voice trembled as she spoke.

"I won't say what it is, and don't you dare look." she told the boy, as two large, black crows called out from the dead limb of a maple tree. She looked up with the boy and sighed as she dropped the small rag in. "He cheated on me with a whore. He was my boyfriend, the closest thing I ever had to one, anyway. He will never do it again. Of this, I am certain." she said, patting the cylindrical package once, with modest affection. Then she patted the boy on the head. "You go on and get this thing done now and hurry home. Your Papa will worry once that storm starts."

She turned and walked away, singing some dark tune the boy had never heard and at last his bucket list had been completed and he headed off for Hollow Creek Road on the south side of town. It was time to face the Devil.

The creek cut into the town like a huge, gaping scar from west to east. The boy found the wooden footbridge his Papa always used to cross over into the woods for hunting and exited off to the left of it, being careful with his footing, and made his way down through the dying grass and weeds to the rocky bottom with barely an inch of water at its lowest point. He turned east and continued on his journey. Almost there. The creek was high above him now, that and a pale, heated sky with not a cloud in sight. He saw many trees with bottles hanging from them to keep away the spirits. He could hear birds crying out and the hum of insects from somewhere in the foliage around him, and far down the creek ahead he could hear something else:

The beating of drums.

They were waiting.

He could feel eyes on him as he walked over uneven rocks and shallow puddles. The snakes, the rats, frogs. The birds and bugs high up in the trees. He was their savior. It all rested on him now, the salvation of this little one-horse town and its dwindling population. When he finally reached the clearing where the creek widened to at least four times its width, he saw them all there on their four corners. The things that beat on that drum and called forth the Darker God.

They were tall and somewhat man-shaped. They stood bent over, their faces hidden by the hoods of their dark cloaks. Their arms that did protrude past the sleeves were ebony black and slick like ink. They banged huge clubs, one in each jet-black hand, on the tilted drum heads before them. They never spoke, they never looked up at the boy, they merely called for their dark master.

Without a word, the boy waded out in the water—which was almost to his shins—to the flat grey rock at the center of it all. He remembered Papa's words about the salt and poured a circle around himself there in its center. He took five black candles and lit each one carefully, placing them around the bucket. Then he knelt down and took a deep breath and over the rumbling thunder and the pounding drums he finally spoke.

"I'm here!" he called out to the shadows and water. "I have the sacrifice!"

The ground shook some, ringlets of water forming around him from the shockwaves, and the drums went silent. The boy watched the water bubble as the massive ram horns appeared first. They were bone-grey, wreathed in moss and mud, and the broad shoulders covered by a flowing purple robe worn threadbare came up next, along with the head. Those bright fire eyes, that long snout that blew smoke like some ancient risen dragon. The smell of death and fear.

This was the time of a Darker God to serve.

"What little one is this?" it finally spoke, after rising to its hoofed feet and stood at least twelve feet tall by the boy's guess. It held a long knotted staff in its left hand with the skull of some huge bull at its tip. Silver chains hung around its neck with teeth and bones. Its red eyes rolled over into yellow as it stared down at the boy. "Are you the giver of gifts this time?"

"I am." the boy said bravely and stood very still, careful to remain in the circle.

"Where is Andrew? Where is the old man?" the thing snarled.

"He's dead." the boy said, bowing his head and at that moment he heard Skip barking and turned to see the small dog come splashing through the water to be by his side.

The great ram-headed thing laughed.

"You have chosen the ultimate sacrifice, I see." it grinned down at him, while reaching for the bucket and examining its contents. "The old man's heart in place of the dog's. You will be greatly rewarded, little one."

"Five good years?" the boy asked kneeling to hug his dog.

"I will give you ten." the thing responded, and emptied the contents of the bucket into its huge gaping jaws and the boy looked away as it made a quick meal of it. "I will deal with you and only you from now on. You will prosper, little one."

"Good enough, then." the boy said and turned his back on the evil thing that slowly sunk back into the muddy grounds. "Let's go, Skip." he called to his friend, the one he loved most, and the two of them, both boy and dog, headed home to a Dark God's promise of better days.

*

PART II

CURSED
THINGS

THE RING

PATRICK BERRY

The person who met me at the Carlos Ciriani Santa Rosa International Airport wasn't the man I'd bribed, or indeed a man at all. Her name was Sofia Reyes and she was a slim, fortyish woman with an aquiline nose and black center-parted hair going grey at the bangs.

"Welcome to Peru, Mr. Pryce," she said, but her dark brown eyes weren't welcoming at all.

"Where is Mr. Figueroa?" I asked.

"He ran into some legal difficulties," she replied. "I was chosen to meet you, instead." From the way she said it, I knew Figueroa hadn't done the choosing.

I sighed inwardly. I'd been awake for eighteen hours and had completely sweated through my shirt during the short walk from the jet to the terminal, across a sun-blasted field of tarmac. A short, officious man with dark underarm stains on his uniform had detained me in Customs for nearly an hour, tapping idly on my passport with a finger as he talked. I wanted a shower, a change of clothes, and a Scotch—none of which I was going to get. "I made certain arrangements with Mr. Figueroa."

Sofia Reyes's eyes flashed with anger. Her thought was so clear I could practically pick it out of the air: *Don't think you can bribe all of us.*

"I've hired a driver to take you to the site," she said neutrally. "The excavation is nearly finished, I understand."

I nodded. "They've been at it three weeks."

"And yet, I knew nothing of it until yesterday," she remarked. "A most unusual arrangement. I understand you're using Chilean miners to do the digging."

"I tried to hire local people first."

She made a dismissive gesture. "The locals won't have anything to do with the Ring. If you've studied its history, you know that. Are you aware of the border dispute between Peru and Chile, Mr. Pryce? It's especially fierce here in Tacna. The people are very patriotic."

"The Chileans will be gone by tomorrow. It's a nonissue."

She gave me a cool look and switched topics. "A word on your excavation. Given your interest in the Ring, you surely know of the Curse."

I blinked at that. In scientific circles, no one calls it the Curse. That term is an embarrassment now, a holdover from 1920s yellow journalism. "There hasn't been a documented case of the disease in nearly a hundred years," I replied. "And we're taking every precaution. Anyone who enters the Ring will wear a CDC-designed antiviral mask."

"We don't know how it spreads. Masks may not be enough."

I was starting to get angry. She knew as well as I did that the disease—whatever it had been—was long gone. "If I get the disease, I'll arrange for private care."

"If you get the disease," she countered, "you'll be in no shape to do anything."

"My team includes a medical man. He can supervise—"

"You have no team, Mr. Pryce," Sofia Reyes said flatly. "In light of Mr. Figueroa's difficulties, we've been reviewing your paperwork. The dates on the permits of your three colleagues were clearly falsified, so they won't be allowed into the country. Perhaps you were late in supplying Mr. Figueroa with the names?"

I glared at her and didn't answer. "Your own permit appears to be valid," she continued blandly, "but our investigation is ongoing. If we find anything irregular that pertains directly to you, we'll let you know. Of course, if you choose to leave the country before then, we wouldn't extradite. Peru wants no quarrel with the U.S. government."

I could have cheerfully punched her in the face. "Duly noted," I said tersely. "If that's all, I'd like to be going."

She nodded. "Your driver is waiting outside the terminal. His name is Hartwood."

"Doesn't sound Peruvian."

She smiled thinly. "No, he's American. I'm sure you'll like him."

The Ring of Yanamarca, known simply as the Ring, was discovered in 1913. The timing was unpropitious: Hiram Bingham III had discovered Machu Picchu two years earlier, and no one had much interest to spare for the smaller and stranger edifice hundreds of miles to the south.

Yet, in many ways, the Ring was the more interesting find. Archaeologists have long agreed that Machu Picchu was an Incan emperor's estate, but the Ring's purpose has never been determined. Its architecture reflects Mesoamerican techniques but not its culture, as if its builders had been inspired by something utterly alien to their experience.

American archaeologist John Lattimore discovered the Ring, assisted by his two colleagues, Dr. Herbert Frenkel and Leland Reed. At first, they believed they'd discovered some sort of ancient plaza beneath the sand: A vast square courtyard of stone, inset with an empty ring of darker stone. The ring was two hundred feet in diameter and eight feet thick, yet protruded only a few inches above the plaza's surface. A worn petroglyph on its flat upper surface depicted an impossibly tall man bending around most of its circumference, his head and feet only twenty feet apart. Between the head and feet was a slab of stone that looked unmistakably like a trap door.

The three men pried up the slab to discover a short vertical shaft descending into a deeper, wider darkness. Frenkel and Reed lowered Lattimore in on a rope. Fifteen feet down, his shoes touched a floor, and when he lit a lantern he found himself in the middle of a tall, narrow stone passageway. The walls were composed of stone blocks of varying shapes: Notched rectangles and polygons fitted closely together in a crazy-quilt pattern. A block set at eye level featured a carving of a stern-faced sun.

The passage had a slight bend to it in both directions, leading Lattimore to suspect that it followed the path of the circle in the plaza above. After informing his colleagues of his find, he began walking down the corridor to test the theory. He found more sun carvings at regular intervals, always on the outer wall. Otherwise the passage was unadorned, a claustrophobic subterranean channel of brownish-grey stone. After three minutes of walking Lattimore spotted a faint glow ahead: Sunlight filtering through the shaft he'd entered by. His theory was correct.

The three men set up camp in the plaza and explored the site more thoroughly over the following week. Lattimore's evolving impressions of the Ring are faithfully recorded in his field journal. At first, he is excited and intrigued by the find, though also disappointed by the lack of artifacts. He theorizes that the Ring is some sort of tomb, and speculates on the existence of a hidden burial chamber.

By the third day, his excitement has flagged somewhat. Meticulous searching in the Ring has turned up no sign of secret rooms. Sweeping the plaza clear of sand has revealed no new entrances, no carvings, no ancient tools. Lattimore still expresses awe at the diligence of the ancient builders—the project must have taken decades or even centuries to complete—but frustration seeps between the lines. Near the end of the entry, he briefly complains of back pain, but adds that it's nothing serious.

The next day's entry is positively eerie. Lattimore talks obsessively of a realization he had while walking through the Ring: Only the sunlight shining through the shaft gives any sense of traveling in a circle. If the shaft were covered again, the passage would seem endless, an infinite corridor of frowning suns. The idea of replacing the slab while still inside the Ring seems to fascinate and repel Lattimore in equal measure.

Perhaps recognizing the morbid turn of his own thoughts, Lattimore spent the entire next day aboveground, performing minor camp chores and surveying the surrounding area. In his journal, he talks happily of sunlight and fresh breezes, though he also mentions that his back pain has gotten worse. An excited addition to this entry, penned later that evening, describes Dr.

Frenkel's encounter with the most famous Ring phenomenon of all: The Butterflies.

Frenkel was working alone deep inside the Ring when he noticed a hovering group of small yellow lights a short distance away, winking in and out of existence. He walked toward them to get a better look, but they retreated down the passage as he approached. When he tried running after them they similarly matched his speed, always remaining the same distance away. Frenkel then tried stopping, but the lights kept moving, forcing him to continue after them.

Frenkel wasn't sure how long he'd followed the lights. There was some indication that he'd lost track of time during the pursuit, as if the lights had hypnotized him. Ultimately he ran out of breath and collapsed on the stone floor, and the lights disappeared. Exhausted, he returned to camp to inform the others.

Frenkel awoke the next morning with a deep pain in his back. By afternoon he was sweating and semiconscious, with his spine curving downward at an alarming angle—"like a banana," as Leland Reed memorably put it. His colleagues rushed him to a nearby Dominican mission, where the nuns were known to offer medical aid to locals.

The nuns agreed to look after Frenkel, but despite their care, his condition grew worse. His back continued to bend, the spinal column protruding obscenely from his skin like the midrib of a leaf. Neither of his colleagues could understand why the spine didn't simply snap. Frenkel died twelve hours later. The exact cause of death is unknown, but his extreme symptoms could have induced any number of side effects. Lattimore proposed that they bury the body in the desert rather than trying to return it to America—a proposal that initially shocked Reed, who found it blasphemous.

But Lattimore had his reasons. His own back pain had been growing steadily; Frenkel's affliction was now claiming Lattimore's body, more slowly yet just as inexorably. Lattimore urged Reed to leave him in case the ailment was contagious, but Reed refused, though he did quietly bury Frenkel while his colleague's condition worsened. Lattimore's final journal entry, written in a shaky script entirely unlike his usual handwriting, read simply: "It's twisting me."

The next morning Reed awoke to find Lattimore missing. Outside the mission, he found a series of footprints and hand-prints in the dirt, leading off into the desert. Bewildered and horrified, Reed followed the prints back to the Ring. He found Lattimore collapsed inside the tunnel, a hundred feet from the entrance.

Lattimore's head was resting on his ankles, his body bent in a near-perfect circle.

A ring.

Hartwood, the American driver hired by Sofia Reyes, was a large, easygoing man with a plump, ruddy face and hair bleached blond by the sun. I'd taken her assurance that I'd like him to be ironic, a suggestion that I'd always prefer Americans to foreigners. It turned out she was being ironic in a different way: *She* liked Hartwood, meaning I'd hate the son of a bitch.

He drove a dusty red jeep with a canvas top, steering one-handed with his left elbow stuck out the window. Fifteen min-utes into the drive, we turned onto a gravelly dirt road winding through deserted scrubland. The only sign of human habitation was a series of utility poles without crossarms, supporting a sin-gle wire at the tops. Shadows from clouds swept over the distant mountains like waves.

Hartwood was a natural talker, telling me—unprompted—how he'd come to Peru in the 1980s as an archaeological stu-dent. His subject was the Nazca, a pre-Incan culture that died out around 800 A.D. I asked if he'd studied the Nazca Lines, a series of animal drawings so large they're only viewable from an airplane. Erich von Däniken made them famous in the 1970s with his absurd theories of ancient astronauts.

Hartwood smiled.

"That's why I picked the Nazca," he said. "I read von Dän-iken's book. His ideas were nutty, but he got me interested in all those ancient mysteries. I thought maybe I could come up with better explanations. But that all went by the boards pretty quickly."

"Why?"

"The '80s were a bad time in Peru. Runaway inflation, flooding from El Niño, the rise of the Shining Path. Most of my studies were in remote areas, so I dealt with the peasants a lot, and they always got the worst of it. I saw one group gunned down by the side of the road by a truck full of men with rifles. The truck didn't even stop—the men just stood up and fired as they went by. Like it was target practice."

"Shining Path guerrillas?"

"Maybe. Or it could have been police. Or the military. I was too busy hiding to get a good look." He grimaced. "After that, the Nazca Lines stopped seeming very important. There's no real answer, anyway."

I frowned at that. "The Nazca had *some* reason for making them."

"Yes," he agreed. "But any reason you came up with would just be a theory. There's no way to prove you're right."

His calm certainty was beginning to annoy me. "Would you say the same thing about the Ring?" I asked. "That I'm wasting my time?"

Hartwood shrugged. "It's your time to waste. But I don't think you'll find a 'reason' for the Ring. Plenty of others have tried."

"I wouldn't say plenty. The last true archaeological survey of the Ring was in 1924. Zapatero's tourists don't count."

Zapatero was an enterprising native who'd set himself up in the 1960s as an unofficial tour guide of the Ring. His activities were strictly illegal, yet he kept them up for forty years without ever being arrested. None of the people he took into the Ring fell prey to the disease, and Zapatero himself died of old age.

"Some of Zapatero's clients were serious archaeologists," Hartwood said.

"Most were mystics and nutjobs," I countered. "Besides, Zapatero didn't let anyone bring modern equipment. No one's been inside the Ring with state-of-the-art gear."

Hartwood looked amused. "No foreigners have, maybe. Plenty of Peruvians have brought stuff in. No permits, of course, so they did it on the sly."

I stared at him. I'd heard nothing of this, not even a hint. "They didn't publish their findings anywhere," I said finally. "Or I'd have seen them."

"They didn't have permission to be there. And there weren't any findings to speak of. Maybe there's nothing left to find."

I gave him a sour look. "I thought the locals were afraid of the Ring."

"These weren't locals," Hartwood said. "Anyway, Zapatero was local. Peruvians don't all think alike."

"But some *are* afraid of it?"

He pondered the question a moment. "I wouldn't say afraid, exactly. They see it as dangerous. Like a rickety bridge, or a patch of thin ice. They think it's foolish to mess with it."

"As do you, clearly," I said. "Did Sofia Reyes hire you to dissuade me?"

Hartwood laughed at that.

"Sofia doesn't play that way. If she wants you gone, she'll be the one to tell you." He gave me a sideways glance and added: "I take it she already has."

I didn't bother to answer. A stuccoed brick building was looming into view on the left, topped by a façade with cast-iron bells set in arched openings. The façade gave the squat building the illusion of a pointed roof. "Is that... ?"

"That's the mission," Hartwood said. "Where Cullum died. And the others."

Cullum, a minor member of the 1924 expedition, had achieved posthumous fame by being photographed in his grotesque condition. No one would believe the descriptions of the symptoms nowadays if not for that photograph. "Is the mission still active?"

"Yeah, the nuns are still there. If you're a praying man, pray you won't need their services."

"I'm not a praying man."

Hartwood merely nodded. "Neither am I."

Wilcox and Cullum were the only two archaeologists among the four-man team that explored the Ring in 1924, and neither man was team leader. That honor belonged to Edward Dunne, a soldier of fortune who'd been banned from several countries for tomb-robbing. The fourth member of the group was a World War I demolitions expert named Perry. Their equipment included picks, shovels, miner's headlamps patented by Edison, and—unbeknownst to the Peruvian authorities—a small cache of dynamite. Edward Dunne was convinced that the inner circle of the Ring housed a secret chamber, where he'd find the treasure so conspicuously missing from the rest of the site.

Compared to John Lattimore and his team of well-respected archaeologists, the 1924 group seems like a band of smash-and-grab raiders. Yet for all the differences between the two expeditions, it's their similarities that are the most striking. For instance:

Both expeditions were overshadowed by finds of much greater import a few years earlier: Machu Picchu in 1911, Tutankhamen's tomb in 1922. Given his dubious archaeological bona fides, Dunne was probably pleased by the lack of attention. Yet the Ring's failure to attract much interest throughout its hundred-year history is puzzling, given its uniqueness and the sensational deaths that have occurred there.

Both expeditions had one member who encountered the Butterflies while alone in the Ring. Cullum saw the lights on the third day of the expedition, and chased them until he passed out from exhaustion. Like Frenkel before him, Cullum was both the first to succumb to the disease and the quickest to die of it. Proximity to the Butterflies accelerated the symptoms, it seemed.

Both expeditions took their ailing associate to the Dominican mission, as no other medical facility was nearby. The infamous photograph of Cullum, in which two narrow beds have been pushed together to accommodate his monstrously twisted body, was taken by Edward Dunne. One day after the photo was taken, Cullum was dead and Dunne and Perry had begun exhibiting the symptoms.

Both expeditions had one member who didn't catch the disease: Reed in 1913, Wilcox in 1924. Each man spent as much time in the Ring as his colleagues, yet mysteriously suffered no ill effects. After returning to America, Reed became a professor of archaeology, eschewing all fieldwork, and Wilcox became a clerk. A comparison of their medical histories reveals no commonalities that could explain why they had been spared.

Finally, both expeditions had one member who, in the late stages of the disease, mysteriously returned to the Ring in the dead of night and died there. Lattimore entered the Ring empty-handed, but Perry brought a stick of dynamite with him. He crawled through the passage to the midpoint of the circuit, as far away from the entrance as possible, and lit the fuse. The blast that killed him caused twenty feet of the corridor to collapse. Perry's body—what was left of it—was never exhumed.

The Jeep pulled up to the dig site just as the Chileans were finishing work for the day. They crawled out of the shaft on an aluminum ladder and plodded sullenly across the stone plaza toward a pair of trailers, like a line of marching ants.

None of them were wearing antiviral masks.

"Get my bags," I snarled at Hartwood before hopping out of the Jeep. Ted Connor was standing in the middle of the plaza, wearing a yellow hard hat and holding a clipboard.

"Mr. Pryce," he said nervously as I approached.

"Why aren't those men wearing masks?" I demanded. "For that matter, why aren't you?"

Connor's prominent Adam's apple bobbed. "I haven't been down in the Ring today," he said. "And the Chileans refuse to wear them."

"What do you mean, refuse? You're the foreman, aren't you?"

"Mr. Pryce, I've had to pick my battles here. Some of the men learned about the history of the Ring. I think the locals must've told them."

"The locals don't like Chileans," I pointed out. "Why would they warn them?"

Connor shrugged helplessly. "I don't know. Maybe they hate us even more. All I know is the workers are mad as hell about not being told up front. If I push them any further, they'll mutiny."

"If they're so damn worried about the disease, why won't they wear the masks?"

"Because it's hard to breathe down there. The air's hot and... *heavy*, somehow. I got woozy the last time I went down, and I was just making an inspection. Doing heavy labor would be impossible."

Damned fool, I thought viciously. If we'd been on American soil, Ted Connor would already be fired, but right now he was all I had left. If Sofia Reyes found out the Chileans hadn't worn the masks, this expedition would be over before it started. "How close are you to being done?"

"One more day. The passage is clear, we just need to do some integrity tests."

"Suppose you don't do these tests."

"Sir? I don't—"

"If you skip the tests, what happens? Does the passage collapse on me?"

He blinked a few times.

"It should be safe," he said carefully.

"Good. Tell the workers to gather up their stuff. Put them all in one trailer and drive them back to Chile. Tonight."

Connor was staring at me. "I don't think all the men will fit in one trailer."

"I can't lose both trailers. Make them fit. Where's the rest of the equipment?"

Connor pointed to a large stack of boxes at the corner of the plaza, loosely covered with a tarp. "Right there. But—"

"Fit the men in one trailer," I said flatly. "Sit them on each other's laps if you have to. Drive them over the border and dump them at the nearest bus station. And if anyone asks—at the border or anywhere else—if they wore masks on-site, you say they did, you understand? They wore masks the whole time."

There was a long silence as Ted considered this, his eyes shifting within his otherwise motionless face.

"Yes sir," he said finally, but I could tell he had no intention of keeping that promise. Nor could I bribe him into keeping it. We were simply beyond the limit of what Ted Connor was willing to do for me. He'd cram the men into a trailer, he'd drive them to the border, he'd keep his mouth shut within reason. But, if someone asked him point-blank about the masks, he'd tell the truth. He nodded stiffly at me and walked off.

The Jeep was gone. I felt a moment's concern for my suitcases, but then spotted them sitting in the dirt near the road. Hartwood must have tossed them out and left. I wondered uneasily how much of my talk with Connor he'd overheard, and how close with Sofia Reyes he really was. He liked her better than me, that was clear enough. But if the Chileans were gone, it shouldn't be a problem.

I rummaged beneath the tarp until I found a camp chair and a bottle of Glenlivet. Unable to resist the gesture, I put the chair in the center of the plaza with the Ring all around me. Some of the workers milling around the trailers gave me sour glances, and I responded with a sardonic lift of the bottle, as if toasting them.

Finally, Connor herded them all into a single trailer and drove away, leaving me alone: One man in a camp chair on a plaza of ancient stone, getting drunk on single-malt Scotch beneath a purple twilight sky.

The original plan had been for my four-man team to spend a month here. Instead, I had no team at all, and Sofia Reyes would probably have me deported or arrested within the week. Yet, here I was. The Ring hadn't been able to stop me. In my half-drunken state, it seemed queerly plausible that the Ring had been responsible for the day's frustrations, desperately throwing obstacles in my path to protect its ageless secrets.

"I'll get to the bottom of you," I promised aloud, raising my half-empty bottle toward the shadowy opening of the trap door.

The next morning, nursing a hangover and wearing an antiviral mask, I entered the Ring for the first time.

Descending the ladder, I found myself in a corridor twelve feet tall and five feet wide. The walls were made of irregular stones painstakingly cut to fit each other, with no mortar in between. I'd seen similar stonework at Cuzco, but here the stones were smaller and their shapes more consistently odd, as if the builders' intent had been to bewilder the eye. The carved suns bore a superficial resemblance to Incan carvings of the sun god Inti, but their faces were considerably more malevolent.

There's no proof that the Ring is Incan. It could easily be pre-Incan—by a century or a millennium, take your pick. Since it's made entirely of stone, there's nothing organic to carbon-date. One of my team members, Heinz, had hoped to estimate its age using radioisotopes, but there was no chance I'd be able to reproduce his methods by myself.

I proceeded down the passage, taking photographs of the walls with a multispectral camera as I went. I soon noticed that the sun carvings had been spaced so that only one was ever visible; the next sun appeared as soon as the previous one had vanished around the bend of the corridor. If that pattern held true all the way around the circle, it implied a remarkable knowledge of mathematics on the builders' part—far beyond anything the Incas were known to possess.

The repaired section of corridor began 320 feet from the entrance, according to my wrist pedometer. Heavy-duty steel mesh, the type used to prevent rockfalls on mountain roads, overlaid the walls and ceiling to prevent further collapse. At one particularly unstable spot an inverted U of sheet metal had been wedged into the passage, creating a tunnel within the tunnel. It wasn't a pretty solution, but it got the job done. The passage had been entirely cleared of debris. I wondered idly where Perry's body was. Surely, Connor hadn't been careless enough to throw it away.

I continued past the damaged area, occasionally stopping to take more pictures. Much as I hated to admit it, Connor had a point about the masks. Breathing the air down here was like trying to breathe hot water. I couldn't shake the impression that the mask wasn't letting enough oxygen in. By the time I got back to the ladder I was audibly wheezing. Before climbing out I checked my pedometer again: One full circuit was 706 feet.

I spent the rest of the day setting up a tent, making a pot of soup, and loading the camera's photos onto my laptop. For the photos, I'd chosen a mixture of visible-light channels and the infrared channel. The resulting pictures looked like a TV having severe color problems, but any ancient drawings effaced by time would be visible in the infrared. I cycled idly through the photos while I ate my soup.

I was on my last spoonful when the grinning demon's head popped up on the screen.

Even as my heart began hammering in my chest, my brain recognized the mundane truth: It was just a photo of a sun carving. The infrared overlay had transformed the stern mouth into a vulpine grin and reshaped the eyes to look calculating and cruel. A random quirk of digital imagery, nothing more.

Except I hadn't taken any pictures of the sun carvings. The whole point of the photos had been to find old drawings, so I'd concentrated on stones with flat surfaces. Yet clearly I'd broken that rule once. At least once.

Well, it was hot down there, I thought uneasily. *Suffocating. I probably just...*

Just what?

Went into a fugue state?

Started photographing random objects?

What, exactly?

The sun's face grinned at me, a mocking leer.

I shut the laptop with a snap.

The next morning, I made two inadvertent discoveries outside the Ring: The slab to the trap door, and Perry's body.

I found the slab lying in the plaza, half-buried in sand. For all I knew, it had been sitting there since Lattimore and his team pried it up a century ago. It's a problem that comes up often in archaeology: This slab was part of an ancient monument, but it was also just a large, featureless hunk of stone. You could put it back over the shaft, but why bother? You could move it to a museum, but who would come look at it? So, in the end it just sat there.

Perry's body—or more precisely, his skeleton—had been stowed under the tarp in a cardboard box. *A pauper's coffin*, I thought with grim amusement. It was hard to feel too sorry for Perry, whom most archaeologists considered a disgrace for his reckless stupidity with that dynamite. Had he thought he was protecting others from the disease? Or had he merely wanted revenge on the Ring for killing him?

Whatever his reasons, he'd put the study of the Ring on hold for nearly a century. Partially destroyed, unsafe to enter, known to contain an American's dead body, and purportedly the source of a gruesome disease, the Ring became a first-class nuisance for the Peruvian government. The best thing to do with it, from their point of view, was nothing. At least until my hefty bribe.

Pushing Perry's remains aside, I rummaged around for the ground-penetrating radar unit, a handheld device resembling a bulky walkie-talkie. Then I descended the ladder and began circling the Ring again, traveling counterclockwise this time for variety's sake, stopping every few feet to take another reading.

It was a long boring job, ironically made more dull by the many positive results. The unit detected numerous hollow spaces behind the walls and floor, all of them small and irregular and probably just natural fissures or animal burrows. I marked each location with a chalk "X" for later investigation. By the time I completed the circuit, the hazy red light of sunset was filtering through the shaft. I ate a quick supper back at camp, then returned to examine the chalk-marked spots.

I'm usually good at sticking to routine, even when the activity seems pointless. Doing a job right the first time means never having to second-guess yourself later. Yet, as I worked my way through the X's I found myself chafing at the foolishness of it. The primary mistake of the previous two expeditions had been to assume that the Ring was merely an anteroom to some sort of tomb or treasure trove, a theory supported by nothing beyond simple greed. I felt suddenly sure that the mystery of the Ring wasn't hidden behind the walls or under the floor. The circular corridor itself *was* the mystery.

My irritation increased when I reached the repaired section of the passage. Perry had been a brainless thug, bringing dynamite into the Ring like some amateur safecracker. The beauty of the Ring was in its deliberate monotony, the way that any given section of the corridor looked exactly like any other.

That beauty was gone now, ruined by scarred stonework and steel mesh and an absurd sheet-metal tunnel wedged into the passage like a curl of paper in a bottle's neck. I'd never be able to see the Ring as Lattimore had seen it: Pristine, unbroken, unending—a passage that went on forever. Put the slab back over the entrance and that section would look just like the rest; you'd never notice it. Go around enough times and maybe it wouldn't even be there, anymore....

I shivered despite the heat, feeling the hair on my forearms rise. These weren't normal thoughts to be having. Something was happening to me. I put my palms flat on the wall and bent my head between them, closing my eyes as sweat dripped from my brow onto the floor.

When I opened my eyes again, the light had subtly changed. My halogen lantern cast a steady white glow, but the light playing on the stonework in front of me was yellow and shimmering. I turned my head to see a pulsing cloud of yellow lights hovering in the middle of the corridor.

The Butterflies had come.

I stared at them in disbelief. I'd brought along a boxful of suction-cup-mounted minicams to record the Butterflies if they appeared, but I hadn't bothered to put them in place. Even if my whole team had been here, I might not have bothered. The Butterflies had always seemed like the least credible part of the Ring legend, usually explained away as a sickness-induced hallucination. Yet here they were, not ten feet from me. The lights bloomed and shrunk exactly like butterflies opening and closing their wings, though it was obvious these weren't insects. I had no idea what they were, but they weren't insects.

I took a step toward them, and they immediately glided away from me the same distance. A direct response to stimuli. I tried again, a slower step, and they drifted backward more slowly as if playfully matching my pace. I frowned. If they moved when

I moved, it made more sense to stay still. But how could I ever close the gap, then?

Abruptly the Butterflies retreated down the corridor, moving faster than before. I had to jog to keep up with them, breathing heavily through my mask. I'd neglected to pick up the lantern, and its white glow was soon lost behind me. I was running through near-darkness, with only the yellow radiance of the Butterflies to guide my steps.

How long did I chase them? I remembered passing through the sheet-metal tunnel early on, but I couldn't recall seeing it again, or the lantern either. Yet, based on my final position I must have passed each of them at least once more. I had no memory of falling down either, yet I awoke on the stone floor in darkness, feeling winded and wretched. My head was pounding and my right knee hurt. The side of my face was gritty from the floor.

I staggered to my feet, orienting myself in the corridor with an outstretched hand. The passage behind me seemed slightly brighter, suggesting the lantern lay in that direction. As I hobbled through the dark I realized I was clutching a wadded-up piece of material in my left hand. It was my antiviral mask. I'd torn it off at some point to get more air.

I awoke the next morning with a terrible backache.

I had so many other physical woes—a headache, a throbbing knee, a parched throat—that the significance of my back pain didn't immediately register. When it did, I paused and sat on my cot a moment, wondering how much danger I was in.

I'd lain unconscious in the Ring for less than an hour, and I'd replaced the mask I soon as I realized what it was, so my exposure had been minimal. I was fifty years old and could've easily strained my back when I fell, or just by overexerting myself. And there hadn't been a documented case of the disease in nearly a hundred years.

On the other hand, I'd seen the Butterflies. Only two other men had ever seen them, and they'd both died within a day.

If I truly had the disease, what were my options? I still had a trailer, but I didn't know the area. At best, I could find my way back to the Dominican mission, to die among the nuns. Or I could call for help, assuming I found the satellite phone. Assuming Ted Connor hadn't driven off with the satellite phone. Assuming the satellite phone had even been packed in the first place.

The sound of a vehicle interrupted my reverie. I arose and exited the tent to find Hartwood walking toward me across the plaza. He recoiled slightly upon seeing me, which wasn't surprising. I was unwashed, unshaven, and the right knee of my trousers was soaked with blood.

"Mr. Pryce," he said uncertainly.

"What are you doing here?"

"I overheard your talk with your colleague," he admitted. "And reported it to Sofia. She's tracking the Chileans down, now. I thought you ought to know."

I laughed humorlessly. "So, you betray me, and then you betray her. You're a peach, Hartwood."

"I haven't betrayed anyone. I kept her informed because I promised her I would. I'm telling you because it would be less hassle for everyone if you just cleared out of here now."

I shook my head. "I'm not going away."

"You'll be *taken* away," he insisted. "Within a day or two. What do you hope to achieve in that time? You can barely stand up." He said it dismissively, but then his face went white and he took an involuntary step backward. "You're bent over."

I made an effort to straighten up. "I fell down. I'm injured, that's all."

He shook his head in wide-eyed disbelief and ran back to the Jeep. I watched impassively as he drove off. As soon as he reached a phone he'd be calling Sofia Reyes. Time was growing very short.

I spent the morning making a slow circuit of the Ring, attaching a minicam to the wall every thirty feet. Even that simple bit of labor exhausted me. When I was done, I staggered back to my tent, tore off my mask, and collapsed in the camp chair.

Hartwood was right about one thing: I didn't have the energy left to accomplish much. My only hope was to get visual proof of the Butterflies' existence before I was done. That alone would secure my legacy. To keep my strength up I ate two cans of peaches and drank a small glass of Scotch, but either the food or the booze put me directly to sleep. When I awoke again it was early evening. I'd slept most of the day away.

I tried to view the minicam feeds on my laptop and was annoyed to find that the connections had been lost. The wireless signal couldn't penetrate the stone of the Ring. Stupid of me not to check that before dozing off. I got up wearily from the chair, then froze in surprise.

My back was better. It wasn't fully healed—I could still feel an ache there—but it was mild compared to this morning's pain. And if I was healing at all, it meant I didn't have the disease.

My mind raced. It wasn't too late to get footage of the Butterflies, but the minicams weren't the way. I rummaged frantically beneath the tarp, tossing expensive equipment aside until I found the cheap-as-dirt video camera I'd only ordered as an afterthought. Then I donned my mask, grabbed my lantern, and hurried down the ladder.

Too much walking would tire me, so I just went back to where I'd last seen the Butterflies and waited. An hour went by, then two. Had I done something special before, to trigger their appearance? Or was it all random? To pass the time, I devised a plan for filming them. I would stay still to begin with, to make sure I got them on camera. Then I'd take a single step forward to show how they responded to movement. If they started to flee, I could just let them go. Or maybe pursue them a little while, but not like last night, when I'd chased them so long I'd lost consciousness. I frowned inwardly at the memory. Why had I done that? It should have been obvious I wasn't going to catch them. Why hadn't I simply stopped?

The hair on my forearms was standing up again. I looked stupidly down at my own arms, now awash in shimmering yellow radiance, and then up at the Butterflies. They were hovering in the passage ten feet away, twinkling at me serenely. I fumbled for the switch to activate the camera and they fled.

I chased them. Of course, I chased them. They'd hypnotized me, just like they'd hypnotized Frenkel and Cullum a century earlier. Only my own exhaustion could stop me from chasing them. My single memory of that pursuit afterward was an endless series of carven suns blooming into view ahead of me, illuminated by the passing Butterflies. The suns appeared to be grinning at me.

I awoke on the floor of the Ring with a light shining in my face. I looked up to see two people standing in the passage. Hartwood, holding the lantern, was merely wearing an antiviral mask, but Sofia Reyes was decked out in a full HAZMAT suit. Her horrified face was visible through the plastic faceplate.

"My God," she said. "My God."

I turned my head to follow her eyes and found myself staring at my own ankles. They were lying in front of me at a seemingly impossible angle. I tried to straighten my back, but it was like trying to bend my fingers the wrong way. I could manage an inch of flex, no more.

I'd caught the disease after all.

———————

They took me to the Dominican mission. I almost had to laugh at the irony of it.

I was laid out on a narrow cot in a white stuccoed room lit by an old-fashioned oil lamp. The nuns who glided in and out were all wearing antiviral masks, probably borrowed from my own dig site. Sofia Reyes kept her HAZMAT suit on, taking no chances. The agony in my back was unrelenting.

"Two of your Chilean miners are showing the symptoms," Sofia told me pitilessly. "Those are just the ones we know about— they checked themselves into hospitals. We need a full list of names from you."

I gritted my teeth against the pain. "I don't know their names. Talk to Ted Connor."

"We can't find him. Where is he?"

"How the hell should I know?" I snarled. "If you want my help, get *me* some help. Actual medical help. Not just a nun with a bedpan."

She didn't respond. We both knew the score: No doctor could help me. We were well beyond the known boundaries of medical science.

I drifted in and out of consciousness for the next few hours. The nuns brought me powdery aspirins from an old glass bottle, and I swallowed four of them. Sofia Reyes and Hartwood argued endlessly in the background, their voices lapping together like ocean waves. My slowly bending body kept threatening to fall off the narrow cot.

At three o'clock that morning my mental fog abruptly dissipated, driven out by a single clear thought: *Go back to the Ring.*

At first I thought someone must have spoken the words aloud, the message was so clear. But the room was empty and dark. The white walls shone blue in the moonlight from the window.

Go back to the Ring.

I could feel the impulse within me, an irresistible urge. It seemed almost biological, as if my outraged body was desperately trying to tell me what it needed. But Lattimore and Perry had succumbed to the same impulse, and they'd died anyway. Maybe the impulse was wrong. Or maybe going back was just the first step, and neither of them had figured out what to do next. I'd need to be smarter than that.

Go back to the Ring.

If going back could truly help me, this wasn't a disease in the classic sense. There were no viruses, no microbes. The antiviral masks and Sofia's HAZMAT suit were completely useless. It was the Ring that had caused the disease. Ergo, the Ring could cure it.

A new realization hit me: The Ring *had* cured it. Yesterday morning I'd had the disease. Not a backache or an injury; I'd had the *disease*. Hartwood had seen it and fled in terror. But that evening I'd been better—not entirely cured, but better. The Ring had fixed me while I slept. Or maybe before that, while I was placing the minicams.

While I was circling the Ring.

My jaw dropped.

That was the answer: Circling the Ring.

It explained everything.

Once around the Ring and your spine started to bend—slowly, slowly. Another circuit in the same direction and it bent even faster. Like you were tightening yourself in a vise. But a circuit in the opposite direction undid the damage. The vise loosened again.

That was why Frenkel and Cullum had died first: The Butterflies had lured them around and around in the same direction, twisting their spines into doughnuts.

That was how Reed and Wilcox had escaped death: Their clockwise circuits of the Ring had, through sheer good luck, exactly balanced their counterclockwise circuits.

That was why none of Zapatero's tourists had ever caught the disease: The Ring wasn't a ring anymore, it was an oxbow. But when the Chileans repaired the passage it became a ring again. And a few unlucky ones had taken the wrong path back to the ladder.

I'd done it. I'd figured out the secret of the Ring.

Now I just had to keep myself from dying.

I galloped through the moonlit desert.

I'd often wondered how Lattimore and Perry had managed to return to the Ring while in such a terrible physical state, but now I knew. Standing on all fours actually eased the pain. And I could run fast now—faster than I'd ever run before, even as a teenager. The ground beneath me sped by in a blur.

I hadn't tried to explain my theory to Sofia Reyes. She'd only think me mad. My theory *sounded* mad. Coming from a living grotesquerie who capered around the room on all fours with his spine bulging through his back, it'd sound even madder. She might even try to lock me in, to quarantine me.

So I snuck off in the dead of night. Like Lattimore and Perry before me.

Getting the window open hadn't been easy. I could only use one hand to lift the sash because the other was needed to keep me propped on the sill, like a dog. Getting through the window had been even harder. In the end I simply dove through headfirst, trusting gravity to carry me the rest of the way. It did, eventually.

I didn't bother to follow the road to the Ring. I could sense its location innately—it drew me like a magnet. Even in the midst of my terror, I felt a mad exhilaration. I marveled at my speed across the brush-strewn sand, at the smoothly coordinated motion of my own limbs. The builders of the Ring had intended this, oh yes. At least some of its victims must have circled it voluntarily, willing to trade their lives for this bestial experience. For the chance to become a human jaguar, however briefly.

It didn't take me long to reach the Ring. The ancient plaza glowed bright blue in the moonlight, a pale square inscribed with a dark circular rune. I scuttled over to the trap door and tried to climb down the ladder, but my arched back wouldn't fit through the opening. It was the same problem as the window, but worse, because I couldn't just launch myself through this time. It was a fifteen-foot drop.

I tried dangling my feet into the hole on the side opposite the ladder, gradually lowering them onto the rungs. *Like rocking a table through a doorway*, I thought mordantly. Once my head and shoulders cleared the hole I simply jumped to the floor, hoping I'd shortened the fall enough to avoid injury. I landed smoothly on all fours, like a cat.

I knew I needed to go counterclockwise—at least two circuits, possibly more. Belatedly I realized I hadn't brought a lantern. Stupid of me. I'd have to travel in darkness. Except the passage wasn't dark. The crazy-quilt stonework in front of me was clearly visible, rippling in the shimmering yellow light.

The Butterflies were here.

I should've known, I thought blankly. *I should've foreseen this.* It occurred to me that Lattimore might have figured out what to do after all. But it hadn't helped him in the end.

I turned and scampered down the counterclockwise passage. The fact that I could still see the corridor ahead of me meant the Butterflies were following, but I couldn't take the time to look. If I looked at them I was a dead man. They would hypnotize me and lure me the other way, to bend my twisted spine yet further.

My only chance was to stay ahead of them. To outrun them. Something I'd already failed to do twice before.

But I can run a lot faster now.

MASTERPIECE

Russell J. Dorn

Deliver documents (3) with item <u>0-VD1888</u> to the
office of:

> BERNHARD ELDRITCH, PhD
> ASHBOROUGH UNIVERSITY, RI
> DEPARTMENT OF ART HISTORY

1
From the Scholarly Papers and Notes
of the Late Brett F. Kaufman, PhD:

I first came into possession of Vincent Durant's self-portrait, col-
loquially called *Vincent's Transfusion* (archived as 0-VD1888), a
mere several days ago, and yet I feel already as if it has impreg-
nated my head with several years' worth of material. For years,
the piece remained a rumor to my skeptical mind. Looking at
it now, lurking in the corner of my university office, I am at
once intrigued, appalled, and overwhelmed by the depth of history and suffering it has come to represent through gossip and
a documented series of ill-fated affairs. Though only four-and-
a-half feet in height, the canvas looms imposingly when placed
upon my easel. Presently standing at an arresting six-and-a-half
feet tall, the portrait infects observers with a sense of inferiority,
myself included. Several visiting students have cut their long

awaited meetings with me short. Though none explicitly cited the portrait as the source of the unrest at the time, I've noticed as every one of them peered uncomfortably over their shoulder (no less than several times) during the course of our conferences.

Though I have delighted in the recent rediscovery of *Vincent's Transfusion,* I find myself ever more paranoid of its misery-saturated history. Contracted to study the piece for authenticity, I find myself in the position few others are capable of executing, and that, too, keeps me bound to the portrait. If not for the curious scholar in me and—though it pains me to say—my lack of confidence in Eldritch[1], I have no doubt I'd have sent the portrait away already, or, at the very least, thrown a sheet over it. For, like the students that have subsequently come forward at my insistence, I find myself disturbed by the portrait.

The eyes, in particular, disturb me—sad and somehow vengeful in appearance, they follow me around my office with a morbid discipline. I know, having studied art extensively, of the common illusion at play. I am aware of the linear perspective, the illusion of depth created by the fixed light and shadows, and yet I feel still as if something else is at play—something unspoken and sinister. I've never been one to humor superstition, but I feel as if my logical frontal lobes are at war with my medulla oblongata. Surely, it is this anciently evolved part of my brain or perhaps the amygdala misperceiving a harmless piece of artwork as a threat, and yet I am, in part, left to the whims of these instinctual, subconscious impulses.

I have been in the presence of a dozen of Vincent Durant's paintings, and several counterfeits, most illustrating impious orgies performed by demons and those with faces stretched wide in a fabrication of ecstasy and agony; others depicting a horrific and colossal monster, a collection of hideous and seemingly unrelated features (tentacles, oddly angled joints, and omni-directional teeth).

---

[1]Bernhard Eldritch, PhD—A historical scholar with interest in Vincent Durant's work, whom I had a falling out with over a series of prints that Eldritch deemed authentic and I knew to be counterfeit.

However, despite similar techniques used in the production of the paintings, and even with the innocuous subject matter of the self-portrait, *Vincent's Transfusion* remains the only of Vincent's works that has affected me in such a disquieting manner. Certainly, the knowledge of the paint used could be the root of the troubling affair, or the fact that the portrait was Vincent's final work. Regardless, it does not matter how logically I approach my study of the subject, or how many times I rebuke these irrational feelings, I cannot shake this swelling sense of dread. This has all but halted my research.

Currently, I find that the historical ownership of the portrait is as much, if not more, interesting (and concerning) than the portrait itself. The string of untimely demises and accidents tied intimately to the ownership of the portrait have begun to seem less coincidental and more purposeful now that I find myself in the position as a similar conduit. I take some comfort in knowing that it is but a primal, superstitious fear and not a logical one, and yet I do not rest without difficulty any longer.

I've rewritten my paper, *Masterpiece: A Brief History of a Cursed Portrait,* a half-dozen times, finding each draft less passionate than the last. Fortunately, I saved multiple drafts and managed to bring up an earlier, more constructive version, though not the earliest, as I found several versions lost or corrupted. Though largely satisfied with this earlier draft, I find myself wanting to sabotage the piece, again at war with separate parts of my mind. Worse still, as I spend my late hours writing and revising what I hope is to be my defining scholarly paper on the portrait and artist, I can't help but think that the humorless, painted lips of Vincent have begun to curl skyward with cruel mirth.

As he stands in the corner smirking, it appears to me as if he is expecting to find a new home soon.

2
Masterpiece: A Brief History of a Cursed Portrait

Artists take their work seriously and Vincent Durant, by any observant historian's account, would prove to be an example of this, not an exception. In fact, to Vincent, an esteemed painter and infamous public figure of the late 1800s, art no doubt proved to be the most important thing in his life; certainly more important than his estranged ex-wife Victoria and even his daughter, Amelia Durant. Even just reading the immediately available microfilm media pertaining to Durant would demonstrate to the researcher that, to Vincent at the very least, it was no wonder as to why he obsessed so. "To create: there are very few joys that can compete with such a pleasure," he'd once said to a local publication that wrote an article remarking on his rise to fame and his then scandalous divorce to Victoria.

Truly, divorce at the time was unusual, but equally unusual was the imagery Durant married to a classic style of art: painting. His depiction of scenes containing devils, monsters, imps, fairies, debauchery, and tortured souls haunted the minds of his audience and, like the "freak shows" popular throughout the 1800s, cultivated an interest by word of mouth and circulating newspaper articles seeking, in varying degrees, to disparage, discredit, and defame Durant. A few psychiatrists[2] of the time added fuel to the fire by suggesting Durant's fascination with the images blunted his love for his wife, and with the support of local religious leaders, attempted to use his shortcomings as a warning to the faithful masses. However, Vincent's fascination proved not to be an uncommon one, as interest in his taboo work continued to grow and distant entrepreneurs and enthusiasts began to travel across Europe to see his work.

Music, film, dance, and sculpting are all ways to produce art, but Vincent was drawn to painting. Ever since his failed attempt at sculpture[3], at which his grandfather had excelled, he'd been fascinated with the more subtle strokes required for painting and the fact that it set him apart from any artist in the family and he no longer had to compete with his own flesh and blood. He pursued his painting education in a series of mentorships,

---

[2]James Schoen, MD, and Mason Crosswhite, PhD, were both vocal opponents of Vincent Durant's and even made a motion to have him involuntarily committed to an asylum for further evaluation and treatment.
[3]Durant dropped out of college art classes in sculpture in 1854. Report cards indicate that he would have failed had he not dropped.

finding the impersonality of college work to be demeaning and unfruitful. After several years of painting commissions and portraits, Vincent overcame the second hurdle of setting himself apart from the colony of other artists, by making a name for himself in an usual way: he only painted in shades of red.

Red Hot—The Fire of the Devil? read one newspaper article on him.[4] The article, like most of the time, had the motive of disparaging enjoyment in Durant's work as there was, even to the layman observer, an obviously sinister aspect to it.

Another read: *Artist Paints the Town Red.*

Durant or Dracula? began another from America.[5]

The art critics adored Vincent's work[6], some finding an apparent and brave challenge to the Catholic Church in the images; others simply appreciated the novel approach to art. Durant twice had to turn down offers to display his work in galleries as he'd already had plans those weeks to be featured in other galleries. Though the populace seemed to love his work, Vincent never could think of any of his creations as perfect. According to his journal, he said (in apparent jest) that he'd more likely side with the journalists and clergy than the art critics, so haunted he was by his perceived failings. It seems that, as time went on, he began to hate his earlier pieces altogether. The more he saw them; studied them, the more he began only to see their imperfections. "The wrong shade has been used here," he'd remarked in a journal entry on a small image of a succubus. The violence of his pen strokes indicates his anger with the mistake. The mere sight of his old paintings began to make him sick, so much so that he'd called upon a doctor to visit him. So, when curators and admirers offered to buy the paintings, he sold them for less than he probably could have gotten just to be rid of them—that is, both the paintings and the buyers.

Vincent had become antisocial over the years. Even brief conversations proved trying. Durant wrote in detail on some of his

---

[4]The Daily Break—July, 27th 1888. Page 2. Article.
[5]The Plain Record—July, 30th 1888. Page 1. Article; and from across the pond: Liberty Tribune—August, 13th 1888. Page 4. Article.
[6]This Pointless Struggle—Page DCLXVI—"What fools to respect such blight on art, on man, on life. Do not struggle any longer. Submit to your shortcomings, these voices tell me, as we all must do."

encounters that go a long way in expressing his mind set. The following is one of the more telling entries in Durant's journal. His final entry:

> "Where do you procure your paints?" a curator inquired of me this evening. As he appeared a learned man with grey whiskers, it surprised me that he knew so little of me as to ask something that I assumed, until the present, well-recognized. A humbling experience or an annoyance? I have yet to make up my mind. "I make my own," I replied. The curator puzzled as if I had given a complicated speech on the matter. A portly man, I imagine he will be analyzing the few words over several suppers, as if there were some hidden quality about them, some profound truth. I had, of course, meant only what the words said literally. It proves both financially responsible and more personal to make one's own paint. In any case, I left the curator pondering to return to my studio. On the ride home, embarrassingly enough, I found myself holding the reins too tightly. My knuckles turned white as a blank canvas. Though at the sight of my own flesh reminded, I considered picking up more paint supplies, I decided against it. Unless I become suddenly inspired, I'll have no need for more than what I already possess. What a cursed existence I now suffer. Do you not agree, Victoria?

According to several scattered journal entries, Vincent had grown frustrated with painting. No matter how much praise he received, he could never feel pleased himself. He no doubt thought about stopping; just pushing aside the canvases and walking away from his artist studio, but he hadn't the slightest idea what else he might do. His art now paid the bills. He'd put so much time into the mastery of painting that he had no other real strengths and little experience in anything of societal value. Losing his friends had been the start of it. His wife had long since left him and taken his daughter with her. Durant had poured himself into his work, so at the time losing them hardly seemed to bother him. Now, though, he undoubtedly wished he even had just one person to talk to about what he was feeling. However, he had only his paintbrushes and his journal.

Stepping through the threshold of my studio this evening, I took pause, allowing an indulgent breath as I braced myself. Oh, truly, how it pains me to see them in my present state—these failings. I lingered for a handful of long moments, delightfully blind, before illuminating the room with the lanterns. Familiar sights of my old works indeed still haunt my walls. The paintings, which had once spoken to me, have fallen into an eerie silence. They make lousy, inept company. I decided to try painting after all, for lack of anything else to do; if only to take my eyes from the walls for a time. The studio hung heavy with silence until the clatter of my paint palette resounded through the room; and now that clatter refuses to perish. I fear I have ruined yet another canvas and let my irritation get the better of me, tossing the palette in frustration. My anger might still be observed in my writing....The passion that once made painting seem to be the most natural thing in the world has truly gone; I said as much to the lifeless voyeurs about the room and say so to you now. I find that I presently struggle to paint even the simplest of images. Every brush stroke is a disgustingly mindful act. This feeling of awareness sickens me. A thought that I've entertained for some time crossed my mind again—the thought that I might as well go into accounting or try my hand at agriculture in some sun sick country. This isn't art. This is a routine. The canvas: a duplicate of all the others.

Before he began work on his portrait, Durant scribbled this final entry that oozed with enthusiasm absent from his previous entries (and references to Victoria's abandonment). He perhaps feared he might fall asleep and forget his sudden passion and thus wrote it in his journal, hoping to spark it again if need be.[7]

> I caught sight of thing [sic] in the mirror a moment ago. It stirred emotions deep within me that I wish to capture here in words, but I imagine I can only but touch at the outline of the vision. I am not a poet, after all, but a painter. In my anger, my face had been stricken with an upsetting red. Inspiration struck, Vic! I've pulled from the cabinet a large canvas. The largest I have on hand—it stands to my chest as you used to. Three-quarters of my height. This is a task I'd never once considered before but presently enchants me. A self-portrait. Might it show you the soul that your bare eyes overlooked.

Though the short passage proved to be Vincent's final entry, there is still much of the story to be assembled from other sources. While I have taken many creative liberties in constructing the following passage, I feel confident in its accuracy. As confident as I might be if I were an actual witness of the incident.

Nevertheless, a disclaimer: the following is reconstructed (in narrative format) from various sources—police reports, supply records, medical records, and gossip from the time[8]:

> In a flurry Vincent adjusted his mirror so that from his stool he could gaze into it at himself as he created. He began with his outline, deciding to start with a diluted, pale red. He got the angles just right. With a fine-tipped brush, he then started to capture the features of his face before his eyes got too puffy from the exhaustion that would no doubt come. This, too, came with ease. Vincent lost himself in the work. For the first time in a long while, he found himself able

---

[7]Durant had taken to drinking excessively to cope with his depression and frustration and frequently passed out in the middle of painting, only to wake after his enthusiasm for a piece had all but vanished.

[8]—and the voices that have eaten the silence like tuberculosis.

to smile. He painted for hours before his paint supplies began to run low. Though he had to struggle to pull himself away from his work, he did so in order to search his cabinet for more paint.

He opened the cabinet doors, scanned the middle shelf, the top; then he stooped to search the bottom though he never kept paint there. Empty. The cabinet was empty. He couldn't bear to spend the time mixing more paint, let alone spend the time traveling to the store to get what he needed to make it. He feared the passion to create would flee if he were to leave his studio or even the canvas for a moment longer. If he opened a door or a window it might just slip out, he thought madly. He had some cheap paints on hand, but the thought of using them disgusted him. Those paints, in his mind, were suited only for practice.

Slamming the cabinet door shut in annoyance, he accidentally pinched his finger in the hinge of the door. He hissed as he sucked air in through his teeth and gripped at his injured finger. The tip of it bled. As he cleaned the wound with a rag and a dab of spirits, he saw how the rag soaked through with such a vibrant red.

It just might do, he thought.

It was as he shuffled back to the canvas that he saw it: a knife. It glinted in the harsh light of his studio. A series of tête-à-têtes erupted around the room from the paintings that had once been so silent. Vincent looked around the room so as to not miss out on the soundless conversations. They were speaking to him again, the paintings. One insisted he use the technique he'd used on the hair of a young woman for his new portrait. Another suggested he use more pressure to capture the vitality so beloved by the critics.

Grabbing the knife, Vincent studied it for a moment: the sharp edge, the glint, the pale bluish hue. Razor-sharp, it wouldn't hurt that bad, he considered. Taking a deep breath, he nicked himself on the inside of his palette wrist. It worked. Blood began dripping from it in little bubbles. Emboldened now, he cut a little deeper, further up his forearm. This gave him a different density and surplus that would be great for painting his portrait's clothes and eyebrows. It was good enough to start, so he picked up his brush and began to paint once more. How rich these colors were; how vibrantly red. When mixed with a little coal ash from the stove, the result was near black.

Vincent found himself consumed with the piece once again. His hand had a mind of its own and every stroke was made with ease and made perfectly. As the piece went on, he found he needed more and more "paint." The cut he'd made had begun scabbing over and stopped bleeding. He had to cut his forearm again. This time, he did it deeper so it wouldn't heal as quickly as the previous two cuts. He found that it hurt worse to break open the newly formed scabs than it did to cut a new wound with the sharp knife.

His entire forearm was red in an instant this time, dripping with fresh blood. Vincent's eyes; however, were torn between the mirror and his canvas. He paid no mind to the feeling of warm liquid dripping between his fingers and then puddling in the crease of his elbow as his arm moved up and down. He was nearly finished anyway. He could spend as much time as he needed cleaning up his studio afterwards.

He felt light in the head and thought it must be what creating a masterpiece felt like. That was until he began to feel quite dizzy and his arms and legs grew weak. He finished his last few strokes on his knees and barely managed to sign the canvas in the bottom corner. After he put his brush down he collapsed onto his belly. His shirt felt wet. How much was he bleeding? He could now feel that his arm was pumping blood, not dripping. It was too much.

In the reflection of the mirror, he could see he had become nearly as white as the canvas had started out as. With the last bit of his strength, he was able to lift his eyes and observe his portrait. It looked just like him, except perfectly red, though he himself had become quite red from the shoulders down.[9] There was blood everywhere, it seemed, except perhaps in his veins. He realized he would soon be dead. Anxiety gripped at him. He hadn't the strength to shake it. At least he had made something perfect, he thought, his masterpiece! He'd put all of himself into it. One could argue that he almost literally did so given how much blood he'd sacrificed to finish his red portrait. He could be content in knowing that he did all that he could to—

No, wait.

There—in the corner—what was that? A shade of red that revolted. It had started to brown. It was no longer red at all, but rather an ugly brown smudge. An imperfection.[10] In fact, most of the picture was in the process of turning brown now.

Vincent would never make the masterpiece he had hoped for. Instead, he created only (what many would consider to be) a cursed painting that would survive to bring misfortune and suffering to anyone who even gazed upon it and an untimely death to anyone who might seek to own and display the portrait.[11] No museum or art gallery would take Vincent Durant's final piece. This might have been superstition, or it may just have been practical, as even the infamous artworks are sought after and targets of theft. Many galleries cited the fact that Vincent's death was ruled a suicide as to why they refused host it. To do so would to be to glorify taking one's own life. Later the piece would be titled, through the whispers of gossip, "Vincent's Transfusion."

---

[9]Crime scene sketch illustrates with shading the extent of bleeding and soiling of his garments and flesh. Identifier: S1S25139029—Richard T. Nicola.

[10]An art critic, Andre Elliot, who had once been a medical student, pointed out the shift of brown to red and suggested Durant himself would have been disappointed in the end result: a brown portrait.

[11]Death records and records of sales of the painting do indicate a correlation between the portrait and death of the owner. Feelings of illness are speculation and have only anecdotal evidence.

At the time of Durant's death, the portrait was inherited by Durant's daughter, Amelia, who had it put into storage. The financial inheritance from Vincent was enough that she needn't sell the portrait despite continual hardship throughout her short life. In 1924, at age forty-five, Amelia Durant passed away from heart failure, having never married. She was survived by no children.

Vincent's Transfusion eventually went up for auction and was purchased by Newt Deemer, a wealthy banker and childhood fan of Durant's work. Shortly after the purchase, Deemer is said to have been struck by a spooked horse, bleeding out before medical help could arrive. His bereaved family sold the painting to an American art collector, Jack Lindsey, who subsequently choked on an undercooked carrot some weeks after receiving the portrait. With Lindsey's final will and testament executed, his collection was donated to an art museum where the portrait was displayed for a short while before being put into the back room for storage. Visitors had been complaining about light-headedness and nausea, and several accidents happened near the portrait. Curators believed collective hysteria was to blame and stored the painting to avoid further accidents and potential legal repercussions.

In 1937, unidentified thieves stole the portrait from the art museum. Little evidence remained at the abduction site. While the night guard was questioned, and held as a prime suspect, he was never officially charged. No suspects were ever arrested for that matter, and the painting remained hidden until the mid 1980s, when it supposedly resurfaced in occult circles. The portrait was eventually discovered by police on a freighter in an unmarked crate and auctioned. It then disappeared for several years in the possession of a private buyer. Every so often, the portrait would pop up for sale at other auctions and estate sales. Last it had been seen in the paper trail was just before it was stolen from a private collection, the owner found dead, stuffed into his oven and cooked as if soft clay in a kiln. The artist in Vincent Durant might have appreciated the form of the dead man, folded into a square as he was. Vincent had always considered sculpture to be a beautiful form of expression, after all.

The number of sightings again diminished before the 1990s, and it had yet to publically resurface again until a few weeks ago during a raid. Several accounts of seeing the portrait had been voiced during its most recent disappearance, but their frequency decreased steadily as memory of Vincent Durant and his infamous portrait slipped from collective memory. An inevitable fact in the golden age of information, perhaps, for there remained only one surviving photograph of the portrait—and remains still, for the several I took, I have since destroyed—even it is known to be a harbinger of illness.

Various groups and researchers have launched investigations into the location of the portrait. Just before I began work on this article, a society of art historians, the Occult Art History Society (OAHS), started the process of following up on a series of sightings, in a joint effort with the local Sheriff's Office. Many of their inquiries and searches proved unfruitful. In fact, with an unusual number of employee illnesses, general misdirection, and a series of accidents, the search was delayed several times. However, during the recent raid of an influential satanic cult house, the portrait[12] was recovered.

---

[12]A photo of *Vincent's Transfusion.*

Experts in the field, including myself, were contracted to help with the discovery, which is why I currently find myself with the grotesque portrait in my office[13].

Both self-professed survivors of the portrait and vigilant historians encourage caution if contact with the portrait is established, as it has been. I can now attest to this advice being sound. It is indeed a good practice to avoid staring too long at a portrait that coincides with a feeling of unease or nausea, and certainly to avoid those that are entirely brown as it may just be this sacrilegious portrait that presently sours the air in my office, bringing with it ill fortune and perhaps even death.

Myth or truth—without scientific study, which I hope to soon begin work on, the world may never be confident as to whether the portrait is cursed or not. Certainly, the leading professional hypothesis is that these misfortunes are the result of collective hysteria, but science requires an open mind. In any case, one thing is for certain: *Vincent's Transfusion* has proved to be Durant's masterpiece, if only by his own definition:

November 19th, 1888

'The masterpiece is death to the artist. The artist must give all of himself in order to create it—he either lives on only thereafter to disappoint or withers away like grapes on God's vine.'[14] —*Vincent Durant*

---

[13]The disgusting scent of iron lingers here. It repulses me as much as Vincent's dead eyes do. As it will you, Eldritch. Even having covered the portrait in a sheet, I smell it, feel it, and otherwise sense it. Only—and this is just as unhinged as the rest of the matter—it seems the words I've written account for my most recent bout of nausea and despair. The pages smell of iron. Holding them to the light, they appear a dark red. As do my fingers. Yes, my fingers are red—smeared in it. I can sense the malignant present in the pages of my *masterpiece* on this *masterpiece*. Masterpiece: what a joke of a word. Truly, it is no longer the portrait that disturbs me so much as it is my own manuscript.

[14]How sweet such release as death would be—a release from these mouthless voices. A release from his curdled breath, his horrid stare, his browned visage taking up space that might have been filled with anything else. I feel them knocking, his eyes, upon my own eyelids the moment I close them; upon my neck the moment I turn away. He laughs—he laughs with those morbidly patient eyes at the heap of waste I clutched so passionately to, as if the writing upon these pages meant anything at all; as if I could explain something so pointless and make it mean something. Only madness might explain how I have come to waste so much of what little time I happened upon on the failing of an artist who miscarried in the creation of his own masterpiece. How

3
Coroner's report on Brett F. Kaufman, PhD:

OFFICE OF THE ASHBOROUGH COUNTY CORONER
333 W. East Avenue
ASHBOROUGH, RI 31893

SUMMARY REPORT OF AUTOPSY

DECEDENT: KAUFMAN, Brett Fitzgerald   RACE: Caucasian   SEX: Male   AGE: 50

DATE OF BIRTH: 06/05/1967   DATE OF DEATH: 07/23/2017   BODY IDENTIFIED BY: Susan Kaufman

RELATIONSHIP: wife of the Decedent

AUTOPSY PERFORMED BY: Nelson Hubbard, MD   DATE: 07/27/2017   TIME: 9:37 A.M.

ASSISTED BY: MARGE GROSS, MD   EVIDENCE COLLECTED: bloody shirt, slacks, blood stained papers, noose. Suicide note in footnote of manuscript.

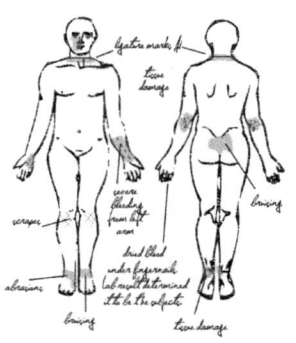

ANALYSIS: Autopsy is begun at 9:37 am on July 23rd, 2017. Body presented in black body bag with 1.5" hemp rope still secured tightly around neck, restricting blood flow. Body is that of normally developed male at 182 pounds, measuring 70.8 cm. Features and state of body congruent with subject's age. Eyes opened. Dozens of vessels broken, resulting in redness. Ligature marks around neck apparent after removal of rope. Further abrasions on elbows, knees, heels, feet, tail bone, and nose indicate contact with the brick siding subject was found swaying against in high winds. Cut along inner left forearm. Likely self-inflicted. The clotting and smear patterns suggest the cut was made prior to the hanging. Note that assistant Marge Gross, MD, has stepped out, citing a bout of nausea and trepidation. Autopsy resumed at 10:15 am on July 23rd, 2017. Y-incision made. Chest plate removed. Excessive bleeding from internal organs. All of them. With the state of the blood, bleeding appears to have been present before the strangulation. Note that Marge Gross, MD, has uncharacteristically, as a result of what appears to be superstition, moved subject's belongings to a box and removed said box from the autopsy room. Marge Gross, MD, asks that I scratch that note as a professional courtesy. Organs removed. Studied sample do not indicate disease or cancer. Autopsy concludes without further difficulty (though not our finest work).

PROBABLE CAUSE OF DEATH	MANNER OF DEATH	TOXICOLOGY RESULT
Asphyxia due to ligature strangulation (A1). Ligature A1 is self-inflicted.	SUICIDE	NEGATIVE

DCLXVI-1351-2017

CASE NUMBER

Nelson Hubbard, MD

SIGNATURE OF COUNTY MEDICAL EXAMINER

---

sweet such release would be, I say again—a release from this pointless struggle to mean anything in a meaningless universe. How many floundering billions are there to crop up in my place and forget me completely, only to be forgotten themselves? If only this cursed portrait could have remained out of my grasp or I had stopped clutching around for this hive of intrusive thoughts, I might have staved off these horrible truisms long enough to enjoy a few more years of living in ignorance. I suppose it *has* revealed the truth to me: there is no canvas, no structure or intent to the chaotic universe, nor to existence itself. Just layers of paint and blood trying to take form on a formless canvas. I have deluded myself too long into believing that Vincent Durant's life was one worth studying, just as I have deluded myself into believing that mine is one worth living. I think I'll hang myself out the window, where I might enjoy a final breath of fresh air, away from his monstrosity. It would be a more merciful way to go than at the slow choke of life's sadistic fingers. Better now than to wait any longer for nothing.

THE LLANO ESTACADO
Mary Fancher

He started at dawn, the clouds flying like mares' tails in the pale light, the air still cool. By noon, the clouds had disappeared and the sun beat down like the Devil's own hammer, his shadow a puddle beneath his feet.

They were six days out.

He paused to rest the burro while he studied the eastern horizon, the direction he'd come from. Nothing but sagebrush and sky as far as he could see.

Turning back to the burro, he removed one of the canteens from the pack on its back. He knew how much water was left to the inch, to the very swallow. With what remained in the other canteens, there was enough water for one more day. Enough to reach the next water hole marked on the map.

Lifting the canteen to his sun-blistered lips, he fought against the urge to slake his thirst. No matter what was drawn on the map, there were no guarantees on the Llano; what was a spring of cool water one day might be piss-all the next. And the old memory that created the map could yet prove as insubstantial as the next mirage.

He allowed himself one single mouthful. Savored it like a fine whiskey and not the brackish liquid it was.

The dog stared up at him from its refuge under the burro, the only shade within miles. Stopped panting long enough to show its teeth and growl.

Blinking the sweat from his eyes, he pulled a tin mess plate out of the pack, covered the bottom with a thin layer of water and set it on the ground.

Make the most of it, you mangy cur.

Then he stepped back, knowing the dog would die of thirst before it came within two feet of him. Because that's the kind of dog it was.

Surly bastard.

When the dog had licked the mess tin dry, he gave the beast a sharp kick so he could remove the plate without getting bit. Refilling it halfway with water, he offered the tin to the burro.

That's all there is, Charley. We got to make do 'til the next stop.

With that, he replaced the canteen and plate, checked once more back toward the east, and continued on.

———————

During the hottest part of each day, he rested for an hour. Never traveled after dark. By late afternoon, he'd pick out a place to camp for the night. Not that any one spot was much different from any other. Out here on the Llano, the land was flat as the palm of his hand, and trees grew only in one's dreams.

Each evening, the sun dropped from the sky like a stone, the heavens and earth merging into a single cocoon of black. He was most vulnerable then, but that's why he'd brought the dog. To alert him to things he couldn't see or hear, things that could be drawing close.

The boy had cried his eyes out when he saw him tie a rope round the dog's neck and drag him away, snarling and snapping. He told the boy he'd bring the dog back, he just needed to borrow him for a time. Even still, the boy made such a fuss he'd almost relented. He was glad he hadn't. He needed the dog for its eyes and ears. For its ceaseless vigilance.

Now as he sat staring into the darkness, he wondered if vigilance would be enough. If in the end, it would even matter.

———————

The map was stained from sweat dripping off his face, the pencil marks smudged by his filthy fingers. He was standing where the next water hole should have been, a blurry X mark on the paper.

But there was no sign of water anywhere, except for the teasing presence of lakes hovering in the distance—mirages that had plagued him since the beginning. His stomach tightened at the thought he might be off-course, might already have passed his only chance of water for days.

His friend Dan Barnett had drawn the map for him, shaking his head the whole time. *It ain't no place for a white man,* he warned. *There ain't no landmarks, there ain't no nothin', so you'll get lost before you know it. Then the Commanches'll git you—if the thirst and heat don't first. The only reason I made it through was I had Amidio, my Lipan guide with me who could read the land like a book. But I'd never go alone. Why d'you say you need to cross the Llano?*

What Barnett didn't know, and he hadn't said, was he had no choice.

It was the old Indian woman the soldiers called "Fancy Pants" who'd told him it was the only way to save himself. Half-Comanche, half-Apache, she was known to consort with the spirit world. He'd gone to her begging for help, almost on his knees. Sobbing for chrissakes out of fear for what he'd seen.

The old squaw was toothless and shrunken, her eyes like chips of flint buried in folds of skin the color of strong tea. Her cheeks and brow were lined and ridged the way clay soil sometimes does after a hard rain. She spoke in broken English, but he got the gist.

A place called El Diablo Canyon in the middle of the Staked Plains. At the bottom of the canyon was a monolith of white rock rising to the sky like a knife. At the monolith's base was a pool of clear water and behind the pool the old ones had painted strange figures on the sheer white rock. He should wait there until the moon was a slash of white in the night sky, then smoke a pipe using the fragrant leaves she gave him and beg 'Isánáklésh for forgiveness. If he followed her directions, by the time the sun rose next day the curse would be removed.

El Diablo Canyon, Barnett had repeated. *We passed near there, but Amidio refused to stop, not even for water. Couldn't understand it myself seeing as how our canteens were running low, but the Indian was spooked and you know how Indians get when they think there's bad medicine close by.* Barnett had looked at him long and hard. *I've heard strange things from white folk, too.* Then he'd shrugged and drawn the map.

He scanned the horizon again, noting where a shimmering lake beckoned in the distance. The same lake, the same distance, every day.

Don't believe everything you see out there, Barnett had warned him. *Believe it when you can touch it.*

He sat down on the hard ground and peered at the map again.

Next morning he awoke sore, his tongue swollen from thirst, his stomach hollowed for want of a good meal. The skinny jackrabbit he'd shot the night before hadn't gone far between the dog and him. His belt was on its last notch, and he could count each rib just by touching. Even the burro acted sickly.

He glanced over to where the hound lay, its tongue hanging down like a loosened tie. The expression on its feral face never seemed to change, making him wonder if the animal was simply unburdened by hardship.

Only the burro, poor Charlie, seemed to share his misery. It gazed at him out of sad, knowing eyes as he loaded gear onto the leather and wood frame on its back, almost as if it had looked into the future and found it bleak. He tightened the load and called for the dog. Began another day's journey.

Throughout the morning, he kept the sun at his back, pausing now and then to look over his shoulder.

At noon, he called a halt and divided up the last of the water, wondered if the worst was dying of thirst and not the thing trailing behind him.

They walked long and rested short the rest of the day, finally making camp as their shadows stretched long and lean behind them. Unloading the burro, he allowed it to scavenge its dinner on the tough grasses nearby while he built a poor fire with handfuls of dried grass and buffalo chips. All the while keeping his rifle close at hand.

He shared a meal of pemmican with the dog as the sun winked out in the west. It left an eerie half-light that spooked him to the core.

What followed was worse—was always worse. He feared the dark. Especially on moonless nights like this when the stars sang, and strange, inky shapes swept over the desert.

He awoke with a start, his ears ringing from the sound of Charlie bellowing in long, gasping wheezes. Still wrapped in his blanket, he grabbed his pistol, pointing it in all directions until his eyes cleared of sleep. Ten feet away, the dog stared intently into the darkness. Then it began to howl.

He immediately threw off the blanket and leapt to his feet. He shot a boot at the dog to stop its howling and calmed the burro by holding his free hand over its nose, straining his eyes and ears to see something, hear something. Knowing how things could change in the blink of an eye.

For twenty minutes, he stayed this way until he convinced himself it had only been a coyote wandering close to camp. Maybe a panther. He brought the burro closer in and built up the fire just in case. Picked up his boot from where he'd thrown it and returned to his makeshift bed.

But he couldn't sleep. He kept waiting for something to happen.

When it started raining next morning, he was sure he'd lost his mind. *Thirst will make you crazy,* Dan had told him. *Make you see things that aren't there.*

I'm already seeing things, he'd wanted to say.

But if he was crazy, it was the kind of crazy that ran off your face and soaked your clothes. He raced to pull the pot from the saddle pack and set it on the ground, then turned his hat upside down, placing it beside the pot. Lifting his face to the sky with his mouth open wide, he thanked the good Lord for one favor, anyway.

He remained this way for minutes, feeling the grit wash off his face and hair, savoring the metallic taste of rain. When he finally blinked his eyes open, it was only to see the damned dog with its snout in the pot. He launched his foot out, but the mutt was wise to his ways and dodged the blow. It held its ground a few feet away with its head lowered and its lips curled.

Still it rained.

When the pot was full, he filled the canteens, then held the hat out for the burro to drink. For forty minutes, the rain came down so hard they were all able to quench their thirst. By the time it stopped, he almost felt tipsy.

As the rain began to let up, his relief was replaced by worry. It wasn't supposed to rain like this in the Llano Estacado. Not this time of year.

He touched his damp hair and clothes to reassure himself, but his eyes were drawn to the east. Maybe the thing didn't want him to die.

At least not yet.

When two days later the burro dropped dead, he nearly cried. He'd had the animal twelve years and he felt the grief like it was his own son lying there motionless. Ashamed to say he'd treated it better most times than he'd treated his own flesh and blood.

For some reason, losing the burro made him think about the wife he'd left behind, and he felt doubly grieved.

Oh, Mathilda, I feel bad about the beating I gave you the night before I left, but you know how it is when the liquor comes upon me. And you don't know what it is I saw that night, the reason I left.

He pushed the thought from his mind as he cut open the burro, carved tough steaks to cook for the dog and him and tried not to think about what he was doing. The dog watched his every move from a crouched position two yards away. Too ornery to beg.

The meat was tough and when he tried swallowing, it stuck in his throat. He gagged, spitting it out. Instead, he set a piece aside for the dog and divided his belongings into two packs. When he was done, he extended the meat in the fingers of one hand, coaxing the dog closer. The other hand held a length of rope he'd looped and knotted. The dog was suspicious, as always, hesitant to approach. Finally, hunger trumped fear, and it moved near enough for him to slip the rope around its neck.

Immediately, the beast exploded in a snarling ball of fury. He let it play itself out, only whacking it once with the butt of his gun when it got too close. Finally exhausted, the dog crouched on the ground and glared at him, hate smoldering in its eyes. Too bad for the dog, he thought. It would have to share some of the burden the burro had borne.

He fashioned a makeshift muzzle with his belt and slipped it around the dog's nose, then divided up the packs between the dog and him. It took a couple thumps with his fist to make the cur accept the harness he'd rigged and the weight on its back, but finally the animal succumbed to the inevitable.

They continued this way for several hours before he realized the dog was acting squirrely and had been for awhile. At first he thought it was the newness of the load on its back, but on closer inspection, he didn't think it was the pack at all. The dog was fussing about something in the distance behind them. In the direction from which they'd come.

He wiped the sweat from his eyes and peered into the spent distance. The only thing visible was the blinding white sky and rivers of heat rising from scorched land. He looked harder just to make sure until his eyes ached and he gave up.

Removing his rifle from its scabbard, he held it close as they walked on, glancing over his shoulder more frequently. It was only when the dog started growling that he halted once more. Barely visible toward the east was a wobbly form so far away it could have been a speck of dust in his eye.

It could be anything, he thought. *An antelope, a bison separated from its herd, another traveler, another mirage.*

He couldn't take the chance. He gave a yank on the dog's rope and walked faster.

Come late afternoon, he called a halt. Half a mile away, a small herd of antelope were grazing, noses down, oblivious to his presence. Antelope meat would sit on his stomach a great deal easier than meat from poor old Charlie, he thought. He lowered his pack to the ground and tied the dog to it, gathered up his rifle and crept slowly toward the herd.

He felt more vulnerable without the dog close by. Still uneasy about the thing he'd seen which might not have been a thing at all. Glancing back, he saw the hound sitting motionless as if it'd been changed to salt.

Ignoring his misgivings, he sank to his belly on the ground. It was against plain common sense to let such easy pickings go, he told himself. You never knew when the next meal would come around.

When he got to within shooting distance, he steadied himself on his elbows and raised the rifle in his hands. He fought against a sudden trembling in his arms. Then he peered through the scope and fired.

The buck he'd aimed for crashed to the ground, while the remainder of the herd fled in disarray. Vaulting to his feet, he ran to where the creature had fallen, his mouth watering at the thought of roasted antelope meat.

He stopped dead less than ten yards from the fallen buck, his heart constricting in his chest. Lying on the ground wasn't an antelope—wasn't an animal at all—but the rotting body of a man lying face up.

He forced himself closer, somehow knowing what it was he'd see before he saw it. It was the body of the Apache medicine man he'd killed in a drunken rage the month before.

That night he'd been losing at faro, gambling away all the money he had to hand and some he'd borrowed too. By the time he left the saloon, he was dead broke, blind drunk, and itching for a fight. The Apache medicine man just happened to be in the wrong place at the wrong time. When he fired his pistol, he'd only meant to scare the fool away from his horse and rig, but in his drunkenness, he'd aimed badly and fired a mortal shot. The medicine man died in a lingering agony horrible to witness, and with his last breath, called down a curse on him. This was the reason he'd gone to seek help from Fancy Pants, the reason he was here now, the reason for all this misery.

He backed away slowly as the dead man's eyes fluttered open, the corpse's leathery lips stretching into a nightmarish grin. Then he turned and raced back to where the dog was howling to the sky.

For the rest of the afternoon, he pushed himself harder than ever, his rifle clutched in one hand, hunger and fear gnawing a hole in his belly.

———————————

It was harder now to distinguish mirage from reality. Beautiful Spanish women beckoned him with jugs of wine and baskets of fruit, but each time he approached, their bodies dissolved into the hot air. Coyotes he fired at turned into rocks split apart by his bullets.

Then there was his failing body. The dog with its hollow belly and wizened face seemed to exist on air, but he was burning with thirst and hoped he wouldn't falter when he'd come this far.

By the time they reached El Diablo Canyon, his eyes had fooled him so many times he almost disbelieved what he saw. Down below the canyon rim, the basin was punctured by an immense buttress of white rock. It pointed to the sky like the trembling finger of an Old Testament prophet. This was the landmark he'd been looking for—a single eminence of stone rising up from the desert.

He hesitated before attempting the descent, gathering his strength for the final push. The strange, wavering figure still trailed behind, edging closer with each mile. The dog was ever more skittish, frequently turning about with its tail between its legs as it cowered submissively.

When they reached the floor of the canyon, it was almost sunset. He was hobbling now, so spent he maintained momentum only by recalling what followed behind. He stumbled about the base of the monolith until he found the wall old Fancy Pants had told him about. Far above, he could see the giant figures carved into the smooth rock—fierce-looking warriors and terrible creatures not of this earth.

The pool was there, too. He plunged into its cool depths, feeling his body absorb the water like a sponge. Trembling with relief, he forced himself to sip slowly out of cupped hands, his universe constricted to this one small patch of desert, this single moment in time.

Only when the sun had fled past the canyon's rim did he finally crawl out of the pool and collapse on the pebbled earth. Out of the corner of his eye, he could see the dog staring at its own reflection in the water, its bones barely covered by its mangy hide, the pack still tied to its back.

He thought of the pipe and herbs, the crescent moon, and begging 'Isánáklésh for forgiveness but exhaustion overwhelmed resolve. He lost consciousness and slept.

Faint light was creeping above the eastern horizon when he awoke shivering, uncertain where he was. He could see the dog down below, still sitting by the pool's edge and staring up at him, its pack fallen loose upon the ground. Confused, he tried to walk forward, but although he felt his arms and legs move, he remained trapped in the rock face of the monolith. Turning his head, he saw a carved warrior, alive somehow and leering at him. On the other side was one of the fearsome beasts, pawing its clawed feet and snarling, but caught, like him, in the rock.

With ever-mounting horror, he cried out for someone to save him, release him from this nightmare. He felt the rock wall vibrate with his screams, but his voice remained as soundless as a dream.

Far beneath him, the dog cocked its head as if it had heard his silent cries. Then it stood, shook the dirt off its coat, and trotted back toward the east.

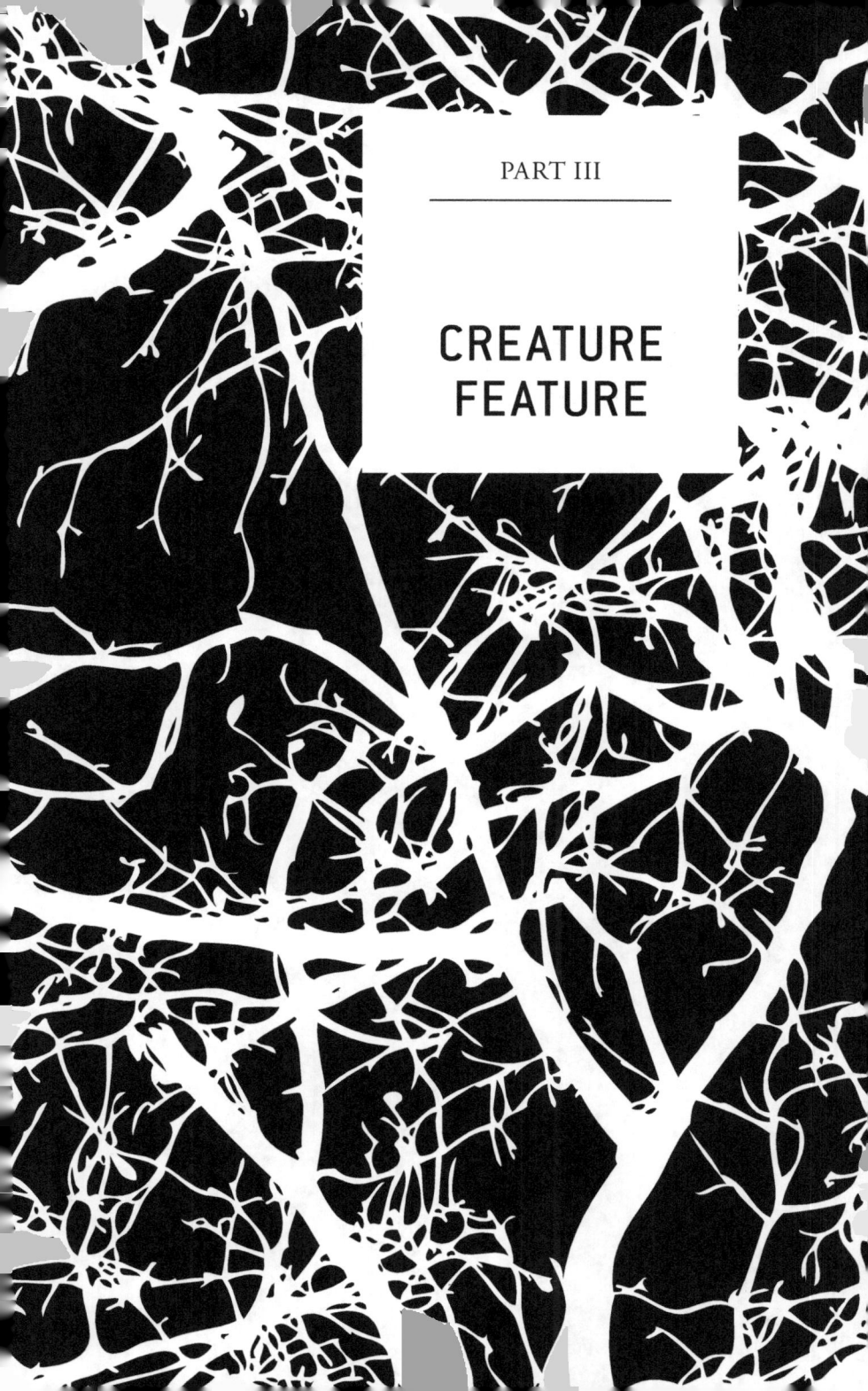

PART III

CREATURE
FEATURE

A CURE FOR NYCTOPHOBIA

ALI HABASHI

It's outside.

I can hear it, scraping one impossibly sharp nail against the tiling on the roof, clinking against the metal bars over the window, tapping at the door where it saw me enter. I don't have a basement, so I am in the bathroom–the one with no windows. When I moved in, it was an inconvenience, something to be renovated in my first house that really should have been done by the previous owners. Now it's my safe room.

I lay the guest towels at the bottom of the tub and curl into the bowl. The slightly stained porcelain is a comfort. Even in the dim glow of the old nightlight, I can see it. The dirty tub is normal: it is expected. Before all of this, it was something to worry about. Focusing on old worries helps sometimes.

I should really clean this before I have anyone else over, I think blandly, forcefully.

I hear a few tiles come loose and fall from the roof, shattering on the concrete of the driveway.

The bleach didn't work. Maybe I didn't use enough?

The bars on my window are too far apart; I can hear the sound of glass being scraped.

Rachel would probably know how to clean this thing, I'll ask her. If she's still around.

Tap, tap, tap.

The towels are damp under my face, where the tears are being dried as they form. I am stiff with fear, my eyes wide and fixed on the small orb of my nightlight, plugged into the wall by the sink.

There is a nightlight in every room and in every hallway of my house, more reminders of things that used to worry me.

Guang had laughed when one of the first things I had done after moving in was to plug in the little bulbs. My husband was well aware that the darkness had been my enemy since I was a little girl, hiding under the covers at night with a flashlight clutched against my heaving chest. I remember falling asleep with it in my arms, like it was a battery-powered teddy bear. Even as a child, I never slept with stuffed animals; all I needed was that cold metal cylinder, with its one warm eye.

Despite the fact that Guang thought my nyctophobia was slightly amusing, he never teased me for it. Every anniversary, he would get me a gift that glowed or shone or rippled with rainbow lights, a silent show of support for my never-ending battle against the dark. My favorite had been a star projector that had transformed our bedroom into the night sky, complete with constellations.

Needless to say, I had thrown it out. The night sky was no longer beautiful, not to anyone.

No one ever really seemed to find out why it all happened the way that it did. No breaking news or presidential addresses broke solemnly over the airwaves in regards to the cause, no accusatory fingers pointed in the direction of the ones who had blindly brought this all about. But I knew what had happened, because I was there, because I had helped to make it happen.

My penchant for all things bright led me naturally to a career in the lighting industry. The sales managers completely ate up the anecdote I told them about falling asleep with the flashlight in my arms as a child, and I was hired right out of college as a Sales Assistant for General Electric. I practically floated up the career ladder after that, stepping lightly over the other employees and the cutbacks and the restructuring at each of the lighting companies that hired me. Sales was a flexible job, and I moved without complaint whenever I saw a new opportunity.

I was a Senior Sales Representative for Sylvania by the time I met my husband in California. Guang was handsome, driven and Chinese, much to the delight of my parents. He was also a Professor of Astronomy with the University of California

Berkeley, an adamant lover of the night sky and obsessive star-gazer. The irony in our romance was not lost on me.

After five years of bleak dating prospects in Ohio, I married Guang only one year after moving to California. We were still on our honeymoon when I first learned about the Dispersed-LED by Omnia Lux.

Omnia Lux had come out of nowhere, an unstoppable start-up headed by veterans from every major lighting company in the US. They were small, but at their glowing heart was the product that had secured their position as one of the top start-ups for that year in both *Forbes* and *Business Insider*. The miracle bulb: the Dispersed-LED.

"I'm going to apply for a job there," I declared as Guang and I lounged on the hotel balcony together.

"Ming, are you seriously job-hunting on our honeymoon?" said my husband, glancing up from his book, chuckling.

"Why wouldn't I be?" I challenged. "Weddings are expensive and we are destitute now, remember? The floral arrangements alone—"

"You are on vacation right now. Relax for a second."

"I am relaxed, this is me relaxing. Look at this, practically all of the stakeholders are from GE's lighting business, no doubt banding together after they were sold off a few years ago. Which I still can't believe, by the way. If Thomas-fucking-Edison founded your company, you don't sell off your lighting business. Tanking sales be damned."

"That's rich, coming from you," Guang smirked.

"Well, clearly they weren't being utilized correctly. I used to work there, and even as an assistant I could already see the cracks. Just look at Omnia's numbers! They are ridiculous, bare-ly a year old and they are already *profitable*. I need to get in on this before they fill out their ranks."

"I am fully supportive and still listening to you, I promise," Guang lied as he started reading again.

I applied that afternoon.

"You are an actual sociopath," Guang deadpanned when I told him two months later that I had been hired as the Regional Sales Director for Omnia Lux.

"How so?"

"You applied during our honeymoon, didn't you?"

"You have no proof," I responded happily, filling out the new-hire paperwork.

The product practically sold itself.

Now, with something as necessary and prevalent as light bulbs, it might seem a simple thing to sell. But just as with anything else, there are hurdles to locking down the larger contracts. No one likes change, after all.

The Dispersed-LED however, was something truly innovative.

Just like the LED, it was energy-efficient and long-lasting. However, instead of the weak directional light of its predecessor, the Dispersed-LED was powerful. More flattering than a fluorescent, able to burn at a lower temperature than a halogen, and even beating out the compact fluorescent bulbs with its mercury-free design, the Dispersed-LED was a force unto itself.

Most importantly however, this magic LED was cheap. So cheap, no other bulb, tube or shoebox light could compare. And as anyone in sales knows, cost is king.

Thanks to a combination of the already semi-developed good reputation of the LED, the government's pre-existing energy laws and a reputable manufacturer in China with a stellar delivery rate, Omnia Lux's Dispersed-LED flooded the market. Its unwavering light poured into office buildings, parking lots, and public streets all over the US.

For once in my life, I felt that in my personal war against the dark, I was winning.

Shit.

It's not giving up. I can hear it testing the walls now, scraping at the pale blue paint. I had my first panic attack the morning I found the first of the scratches on the outside of the house, raw wounded wood scored so deeply that I could see the insulation swelling from beneath, pale pink and tender. Like exposed muscle.

Who the hell do you even call to fix something like this, I had thought as I hyperventilated.

God, I think there must be more than one. There has to be, it sounds like the scraping is coming from everywhere. They never hunted in packs before, but they are getting desperate now, more aggressive. Seems the overhunting is starting to backfire already. Soon they will shrink again, become the emaciated and unnoticed things that they were before, perhaps even more so.

I relish this thought, cling to it even as the window is abandoned and I hear part of the roof cave in under the pressure of the pricking points.

I should probably get on with it, there's not much time left.

I had been working late pretty often since I had gotten the job with Omnia Lux, especially since the company had begun to peddle its product worldwide, but Guang never seemed to have any problem with it. So it was unusual when, one evening, he mentioned it.

"Ten o'clock is a bit late, don't you think?" There was something flat in his voice, like he was trying to tease me but the inflection wasn't there.

I had flopped facedown on the sofa as soon as I got back home, and stared at him over the arm of the couch in confusion at his comment. His face was aglow as he stared at his computer screen, and I realized suddenly that the lights weren't on in the room. The Dispersed-LED bulb from the hall had served just fine for a base layer of illumination, and I smiled inwardly at my product.

With some effort, I heaved myself up again and went to flick on the light.

"Don't."

I turned to Guang, and saw with some concern the strained look on his face and the crinkling of his smooth brow.

"What is it?" I asked, finger hovering over the switch.

"Please," he said, trying to smile. The smile was also wrong, like his teasing had been. I pulled away from the light switch and went to him, perching on the back of the overstuffed chair where he was sitting.

"You okay?"

"It's probably nothing," he laughed airily. God, even the laugh wasn't right.

"Tell me," I demanded, pressing my lips to the top of his head. He sighed.

"One of my colleges—Annie—just got back from the Keck telescopes in Hawaii and she mentioned some...concerning things about the observation."

"Bad data?" I guessed.

"Not only that. Her results were impossible. Half of the data just wasn't there, like at all. She told me that the weather was clear the entire time, and that the instrument specialist couldn't find anything wrong with the telescope."

"Human error?" I shrugged.

"The stars were missing."

In hindsight, that sentence was probably the most ominous thing Guang had ever said to me, but at the time I was too exhausted to even notice.

"So, she was drunk, then," I grinned.

"No, Ming, listen. There are specific stars that each of us observes, and three of hers were gone. Then she went back the next night and they were back, like nothing happened. Annie's one of the best we've got, she wouldn't have made an error like that, and she doesn't drink so you can stop mime-drinking."

"Your instrument specialist is a fraud. It's the telescope," I declared. "The telescope that you use is in Chile, and missing stars shouldn't be a problem there, right?"

"Oh god, I hope not."

"Good, in that case, shut the laptop and come to bed. I'm sleepy." I nuzzled into his hair until he was laughing, and then watched patiently as he stood and left the room. As Guang disappeared around the corner, I flipped on the light and went to get a glass of water.

If I was being too flippant about Guang's concerns, then it was only because I was occupied with my own. The Dispersed-LED, as perfect a product as it was, nevertheless was causing some trouble simply by virtue of being so powerful. Wherever they were installed, it seemed that *someone* nearby was not happy about it. The streetlights especially were pissing people off, their glow bleeding through the blinds and drapes on peoples' windows and keeping them awake at night.

It is not as though they were exceptionally brighter that any other bulb already on the market, but their wider range—combined with the fact that some of the LEDs they were replacing had before only emitted a very weak light—was causing upset. Complaints were never good for business, and I was slightly concerned that my sales may take a hit when all of the bitching finally came to a crescendo.

On the fringes of the public whining were the protest groups, mostly made up of stargazers and night-sky enthusiasts like my husband. Thanks in part to our global outreach and competitive discount rates, decent lighting had been installed in places that hadn't been lit before. The light pollution, they said, was worse than it had ever been.

In the most professional way possible, Omnia Lux responded to these concerns with the following: light pollution is bullshit.

The ocean, the earth and the air: that was the pollution that we needed to be concerned about, the pollution that was slowly but surely killing us all. Just because some of the brighter cities made it hard for people to see the stars at night didn't mean that anything was *polluted*. It was just different. Omnia Lux even backed up this philosophy by donating to several notable conservation efforts.

In the end, our marketing department proved that they were just as ruthless as our sales team.

Almost as soon as the population's ire began to turn on us, the Internet was spammed with articles about the positive effects of the Dispersed-LED. The articles were a strategic masterstroke, disguised as reports on the falling crime rates in major cities and the reduced number of car accidents and pedestrian fatalities. The product's wide radius and long-lasting design had resulted in streetlights banishing even the darkest shadows on sidewalks and on roads across the US, ensuring far safer routes for the residents, both in the car and out of it.

At around that same time as the articles, every major department store and online shop began to stock and sell blackout curtains in bulk. Target, IKEA, and Amazon shamelessly advertised the product after initial complaints had gotten loud enough to reach the mainstream media.

The public's residual complaints were of course a nuisance, but the choice was clear. Either homeowners invested in blackout curtains, or else condemn themselves to the dark and the dangers that came with it.

Too bad good news doesn't sell, I thought as I saw that the latest articles on Omnia had been lost under a barrage of breaking news on the recent disappearances of several noted television personalities, musicians and politicians. Foul play was suspected, and the media absolutely adored foul play.

Nevertheless, the initial dissent had quieted. Time went on, and Omnia Lux went global. In my own mind, the darkness had never seemed so vulnerable.

"Your stupid light bulb is making it impossible for the department to order any replacement blackout curtains. They are sold out everywhere," mentioned my husband, tucking his passport back into his pocket and shouldering his carry-on bag.

"I'll get you some for your birthday."

"Ming, I refuse to believe that you would ever buy anything that might make a room darker."

"I'll take that as a compliment," I sniffed royally. "And as the self-proclaimed Ambassador of Light, I will nevertheless grant you one set of birthday blackout curtains. Providing of course that you accept the Dispersed-LED as your new god."

"That name doesn't make any sense, you know. Diffused-LED is more accurate, they are two different kinds of light reactions."

"Oh please, 'diffused' sounds like something you do to a bomb. It would never sell."

"Please don't say the word 'bomb' so loud while we are at the airport," Guang pleaded as he turned around and kissed me quiet. "I'll see you in a few weeks."

"Have fun in Chile. If the stars disappear, come straight home," I said, mock-seriously as he started through the security line. "We can make some new ones out of my *Dispersed*-LEDs."

"Diffused!" he joked back as he zigzagged through the line. The TSA agent checking IDs glanced up at the word and glared at Guang suspiciously.

Our hold on the global lighting market was all but assured by that point. Even in its youth, Omnia Lux had assumed the role of leader of the industry, and had acquired several smaller companies to support its steadily growing operation. Since I had first been hired, the company had become a behemoth, and had expanded into other industries like tech, green energy, power and had even flirted with travel and nonprofit.

Ever since the light pollution debate, Omnia Lux had also become a huge advocate of charity, assuming—of course—that any and all generosity would eventually lead to profit. They had set up several key locations with graciously donated lighting fixtures, thereby triggering another wave of positive press as well as several more converts to the Dispersed-LED.

Not that it matters, I thought, slightly bitter. Our latest round of charity had gone completely unnoticed once the story broke on the Taken. As it turned out, the constant media coverage on the vanishing of the rich and famous over the last few years had completely overlooked one very important fact.

It wasn't just prominent figures going missing in the US; it was *everyone*.

From every walk of life, from every race, from all over the country, people were being spirited away. A phenomenon that the scientists were calling an anomaly, and the religious were calling the Rapture. As usual, it seemed as though the faithful were winning out. The churches overflowed. Family members cried in devastated confusion during each new report, not seeming to know whether to reach out to their missing loved one, a kidnapper, or God Himself.

When mass disappearances began to occur outside of the US, the beginnings of hysteria began to creep into the reports.

Insane conspiracy theories suddenly became viable hypotheses, when no logical explanation immediately became apparent. Politicians were, of course, the most suspected group in every country, but alien abductions became a close second when more than one witness claimed that they had seen someone dragged into the sky. In most cases, these statements were glossed over as false memories due to mental illness or shock.

Other than the overwhelmingly miserable state of the Taken and their families, life continued. Thinking about it now, I know it seems obvious that we should have all been preparing for the worst, but when tragedy sidesteps you, it is extremely difficult to keep it in your peripheral vision. All I knew was that the news was bad, my sales were good, and my bathtub was dirty.

Still, I can't plead total ignorance.

I came home from a conference the day my husband got back from his observations in Chile. I stood frozen in the doorway, watching him pace back and forth and run his hands over his arms, like he was trying to rub away a shiver. His eyes were puffy, his outfit rumpled, and I could see the sweat stains even from across the room.

Even in the dark.

There were no lights on in the entire house, save for my will-o'-the-wisp nightlights that dotted the walls. I felt the darkness pressing in, suffocating. My anxiety spiked and I flung my arm out and groped at the wall in a near panic before I felt the switch under my palm.

My husband stopped pacing abruptly and we stared at each other for a moment. Suddenly, he started forward with such intensity that I took a step back. I saw Guang's face crumple into relieved sorrow just as his arms fastened firmly around me.

"I missed you, too," I gasped, my face twisting at the odor of his sweat. I forgot about the smell the moment his shoulders started to lift and fall with soft sobs. Stunned, I remained where I was, trying and failing to remember when I had seen Guang cry before that moment. Finally, he pulled back and took my face gently in his hands.

"You're alive," he smiled.

"Huh?"

"You didn't respond to any of my messages."

"Oh, that," I snorted in relief. "I dropped my phone the other day and completely destroyed the screen. I've been using my work one since then. Since I was at the conference I haven't had much time to check my personal email lately, either. Did you really think I was dead?"

"Yes, haven't you been watching the news? New people go missing every day. Hell, they've started using line graphs to keep up with the disappearances throughout the week. Speaking of, come here—"

He grabbed my hand and pulled me over to his laptop, his latest data already displayed on the screen.

"Don't you want to shower and sleep first?"

"No, I need to show someone this. I need to talk this out or I will never get to sleep."

I sat down next to him and pouted at the monitor. The graph, with its four jagged lines arching across the screen, was familiar—something that often appeared in my husband's lectures that he sometimes practiced for in front of me. The axes were labeled *Photoelectrons* and *Wavelength by Microns*—and I suspected that both of them foreshadowed my impending boredom.

"Remember how I told you about Annie's observations in Hawaii?" he began, leaning forward so that I could see exactly how bloodshot his stare had become. "Well, things were similar in Chile. Again, clear weather, working telescope, but my data isn't making any sense. I observe in the optical, using wavelengths as represented by this graph. Now, these spikes that jut up towards the top of the graph are expected: those show up when a star flickers or there is some unusual particle in the atmosphere. You're never going to get a completely smooth line going all the way across the graph. But look where the line dips in these places here: that's not normal. It's like a cosmic ray, but inverted. Somehow, I was getting *less* light."

I stared at the points where the line graph suddenly plunged before spiking back up. Even to my untrained eye, it looked wrong.

"Once might have been fine, maybe twice, but it kept happening. I was getting so frustrated that I finally just got up and left the observatory. I walked outside and I looked up and there was...*something*. I don't know. Something in the sky. It was enormous, Ming. Huge and dark and it almost looked like a cloud, but the shape was all wrong. It was in front of the stars. It was blocking almost all of the light from the stars."

"Jesus, Guang," I laughed weakly. "Please don't tell me that the conspiracy theorists were right about the aliens."

"It wasn't a ship," he said. It should have been a joke, but his eyes were so wide and pleading that I couldn't even pretend it was one.

"How do you know?" I asked, instead.

"Because, I watched it for hours, Ming. It was headed for Antofagasta, the city I had just come from. It was too big, and I can't be totally sure, but...just the way that it moved. I think it was *crawling*."

Neither of us slept very well that night. Guang had continued to describe the way in which the dark shape had reached across the sky towards the beacon of the city even as I ushered him into our room and encouraged him into bed. The next day, he slept well into the afternoon, and when he woke up, he did not bring it up again. I think he must have sensed my disbelief, or else realized that what he had told me was impossible.

A week passed us by, and we coexisted together in a state of tense familiarity. From the outside, I'm sure we seemed perfectly normal. But, lying in bed at night, I could feel the stiff stillness in my husband as I held him. I wondered when the creatures in the sky would find their way back into conversation, or if we would both continue to willfully avoid the issue.

The decision was made for us when not long after Guang's claim, security footage from one of the Taken went viral. Maxwell Barns had been walking home alone after a night out, and had stopped to check his phone in front of a department store. One moment, he stood staring at the little glowing rectangle in his hand, and the next he was dead, impaled on something long and black and far, *far* too sharp. It had driven into his back and out through his stomach, and for one horrifying second of footage, you could see his eyes widen in surprise, before he was suddenly jerked up and away from the earth. Like an afterthought, his phone falls a moment later, bright screen shattering on the concrete.

Like a dam bursting, suddenly clips were appearing all over the Internet, of people being impaled and ripped away from the ground. All instances took place at night. In response, politicians began to back a national curfew and encourage extra safety measures, like installing bars on our windows. The president promised that he would keep the American people informed as soon as it was discovered what was behind the deaths. Nevertheless, it was WikiLeaks that ultimately provided the answers.

A collection of satellite images that had been kept from the public were released all at once, published first on WikiLeaks and then on every subsequent news source's front page.

Creatures. Monstrous, terrifying, gargantuan *creatures* clung to the invisible barrier of our atmosphere and swarmed over it, their features difficult to distinguish even in the sharpest photos. Despite this, there was no doubt in anyone's mind that these beings were responsible for the disappearances. In one of the clearest satellite images, a splayed hand had been captured, fingers crooked like the long legs of a spider, the tips tapering into points so sharp that they seemed able to pierce the sky itself. The middle finger was longer and thinner than the others, with far more joints. If possible, it seemed to narrow into an even sharper point. This curved claw was the only thing that we recognized: the weapon used to skewer our Taken.

Hundreds of names, scientific and otherwise, were suggested for the unknown species. In the end, the one that stuck was *Crux*.

People began to fault the Cruxes almost immediately, not only for the recent disappearances, but for every unexplained missing person or group that had ever been entombed in mystery. From the Mayans to the Roanoke Colony to Malaysia Airlines Flight 370—the creatures were blamed. There was no proof, but speculation on the past seemed to be a kind of therapy for what was occurring in the present.

No one was qualified to state exactly what the Cruxes were or how they worked, so, naturally, everyone tried.

Some pointed out that they were nocturnal, because they only hunted at night. In fact, the monsters seemed to avoid the sunny side of the earth altogether, which made others guess that maybe they were sensitive to the sunlight or could not survive in it at all. This theory only became more viable when NASA, straining to rebuild its reputation in the wake of continuous accusations of negligence, announced that the reason the Cruxes had not been discovered was because they occupied the least-studied layer of the Earth's atmosphere—the mesosphere. Clambering through the air above the stratosphere, there was nothing to protect them from UV rays.

Critics responded with the satellite images, asking how it was that the Cruxes were so visible now, asking where they could have possibly hidden in order to escape detection this long.

In one particularly disturbing photo, a face was partially visible in the frame. A vague slit of a mouth housed jagged shadows that could only be black teeth, while the wide fanning ears seemed almost human in their shape. Its dark eyes were wide and empty, like two tunnels to nowhere. People fixated on the teeth, those telltale signs of a carnivore.

Especially after the latest video from the International Space Station managed to catch one of the creatures as it clawed its way slowly around the earth before briefly slipping into the stratosphere, close enough to swallow a plane. Several openings on its back gaped and squeezed shut in what was assumed to be part of the complicated jet propulsion system that kept it afloat. It moved very slowly, one curled arm unfolding, joint over joint until its death finger was in range of the earth's crust. Then it retracted the arm, and before it folded the 30-mile appendage once again, it brought the finger to its mouth.

The Cruxes, the *things* that took, they were eating the people they stole. Like a predator perched on an anthill, or clinging to the rotten bark of a termite-infested log, we were the populous protein skittering just below. To be consumed en masse.

Despite the horrifying promise of their razor mountain teeth, it was their eyes that I couldn't shake from my nightmares. They were the deepest darkness I had ever known. They were everything that scared me.

The rest of the creatures' bodies were a mottled black and grey and slightly transparent, and so had been camouflaged in the night sky. The light pollution, came the conjecture, was what had rendered them visible.

"That's not right," said Guang, eyes fixed on the television where the latest panel of non-experts discussed the Cruxes. "Astronomers would have seen them at some point, spy satellites or NASA or *someone* would have picked up on the fact that these things were out there. The reason that we are seeing them now is because they are *bigger* than they were before, and not only that but they are in more places. That *has* to be the reason, if one had crawled in front of our telescope before, we would be able to explain it away if it was smaller and moved more quickly. Now they are too massive and slow, and there's no way to miss them anymore. But why *now?* Why are they taking more of us now?"

The military response was a depressing spectacle. For a time it brought the country together, united under a common goal, against an undeniable enemy. All commercial flights were suspended to make room for the United States Air Force. Russia and China also mounted an offense, and, for a time, there was hope.

The world watched as the Cruxes retreated to the mesosphere, out of range and in the perfect strategic position to spear the new delicacies out of the sky. Unwittingly, we had become a delivery service—Air Force à la carte.

Missiles were the next and most desperate step. After the Air Force debacle, the public heard much less about what was certainly looking like humanity's last stand. Reporting was vague at best, untrue at worst, more in an attempt to curb panic than to actually inform anyone of anything.

The most detailed report was the one that damned us all.

Evidently, I was not the only one disturbed most by the black hole eyes of the Cruxes.

In the frantic search for answers, there were droves of biologists attempting to study the monsters from afar. Despite the impossibility of this task, the pictures and video footage had allowed for some hypotheses to be formed on the nature of the Cruxes.

By comparing the eye-size to the circumference of their heads, and then studying the average distance between the Cruxes and their hunting grounds, the scientists had made a strange discovery.

The Cruxes could not see in the dark.

While it had been immediately obvious that their large eyes were neither the grid pattern of an insect nor indicative of an animal with slow photoreceptors like a toad, it was discovered that they also did not seem to have the mirror-like *tapetum lucidum* that let cats see in the dark.

So, that left their size—which, when compared to the distance they were expected to see—simply did not add up.

Which meant that although they were nocturnal, they needed light to hunt.

And what better light to assist them than the Dispersed-LED?

Everything that was happening was because Omnia Lux had started selling the Dispersed-LED...because *I* had started selling the Dispersed-LED.

The creatures were bound to the darkness, and the recent gluttony that had finally forced us to take notice of these otherworldly, almost Lovecraftian nightmares overhead had only occurred once we had lit up the world. There were no shadows left to hide in, no dark corners to conceal, no black streets on which to mask our presence.

It was not the creatures that had lost their camouflage thanks to the rising levels of light pollution: it was us. The monsters above had existed by prodding around in the dark, taking what they could and yet remaining small enough to go unnoticed, and now in our floodlit streets, we had given them the means to become *real* hunters. We had given them a spotlight, shining directly on their prey.

In my endless fight against the dark, it seemed as though I had finally won.

My husband said nothing. The reports never placed the blame squarely on Omnia Lux, only on light pollution itself, so maybe Guang didn't realize what had happened. What I had done.

But I think he did.

Guang was taken on a Wednesday.

By then, protests had cropped up all over the country in response to the government-mandated curfew and suspension of commercial flights, and the national outcry had continued to see people leave the safety of their homes at night despite the satellite photos and videos of the Taken. People continued to eat, drink, and be merry *despite* the new horror.

My husband was not doing any of that when he was taken. He was not attempting any political statement or willful ignorance or show of stubborn bravado. Guang was only trying to take out the trash.

"Guang!" I said, struggling with the overflow of recycling. I watched him heave the black bag into the can and turn towards me. A smile began to form on his lips as he saw me wobble under the blue box, attempting to balance a few empty cartons with the side of my face.

He took one step toward me, and then he was pinned—a butterfly in a display case. The black spike that had driven through one of his shoulder blades was inescapable, as indisputable as a wrought iron coffin nail hammered into place.

Guang's eyes were still on mine, his mouth hanging open in shock and in pain, and then he was gone. I dropped the recycling and gaped, staring at the place he had been, then at the darkening sky where he had been taken. My husband's infinite grave spanned overhead—starless, crawling, hungry. The injustice of it all was agonizing.

The dark sky protests and night crowds have dwindled now, for obvious reasons. Those of us left either live in very remote places, or else have become dependent on curfews. After Guang was taken, I turned over my resignation to the managers at Omnia Lux, and submitted a full report on my light pollution theory. I'm not sure if anyone has read it, or if anyone ever will.

There goes the glass on my window downstairs, punctured through.

Go away. *Please* go away.

I miss my old life. I miss Guang. God help me, I miss the dark.

My old foe. Now, my protector. I'm sorry. I'm sorry for the Dispersed-LED. I'm sorry for the flashlight. I'm sorry for my nightlights.

I heave myself out of the towel-padded bathtub and towards the radiant sphere—my lovely little pollutant. I curl my fingers around the nightlight, and wrench it out of the wall.

And the dark and I embrace, as the world falls around us.

✻

GUARDIANS

Nuzo Onoh

I

My father is a monster, just like his two grey men. They fill me
with great loathing and fear, so much so that my days are ruined
and my nights are dire. I sense their shadows around me, dark
shadows that brim with malevolence, shadows that feel like poisonous fog to my desperate mind. Even now, as I watch the pale
sun of the early autumn dawn break feebly through the grey
skies, I know that the arrival of the new day will grant me little
respite from my long and terrible night. It would just be another
day to hide, another day to wait, another day to tremble with
loathing and terror as I seek a way to end my deadly siege.

The ground I tread on this crisp October morning is not the
familiar surface of my African homeland, but a soft, rainbow
carpet of beautiful gold, red, and yellow leaves, chased from
their tree homes by a jealous wind-god. The dew on the fallen
leaves glitters like tiny diamond eyes while the early morning
breeze sends shivers deep in my bones. Goosepimples litter my
skin, both from fear and from the cold English weather so different from the warmth I left behind in my African home.

Had we been at our village of Mbaleyi, I might have gone to
Mama's cemented grave with the white consecrated cross and
begged for her protection, even though she failed to protect herself from her husband and his two evil companions when they
came for her in my childhood days.

But who knows? Our people say that the weak become power-ful ghosts when they have a wrong to avenge. With what I now know about my father, I have little doubt that Mama's vengeful ghost had a hand—several hands—in his present dire plight.

Except that his plight has now become my doom and I am lost in a strange land, a white man's land so far away from my ances-tors I might as well be on the moon. My only hope of survival rests solely with me, a young man still in his teenage years, alone and friendless, trapped in a dark nightmare that seems to have no ending. Unless I kill my father and destroy his evil compan-ions—*if I can, if they will let me.* Even now, I fear they know my mind, every intimate thought that has passed through my head. I sense their influence growing with each day that passes. The cold October nights seem to infuse them with a blazing power that dogs my every breath. I hear their hissing whispers in the crackling leaves beneath my feet as I traverse the deserted park with its naked trees, bereft of their green leafy clothes. I stare at the tall mossy pines and stark skeletal boughs of the autumn trees without seeing them, such is the fear that cloaks my soul as I think of the evil that is my father. In my mind's eye, I see him on his sickbed at our rented accommodation, his drawn curtains ensuring his room remains shrouded in the darkness that feeds his malice. Everything about him appears feeble and ancient; everything except his eyes, his cold eyes that blaze with greed and cunning, eyes that I used to love and trust till they revealed their true nature to me, the nature of the beasts that lurk beneath the corrupt soul of the man I once called "Papa".

II

I was twelve years old, almost thirteen years, the first time I discovered the two grey men hiding underneath Papa's low bed with its wire-meshed springs that squeaked when one sat down upon it. At the time, I was recovering from a painful cir-cumcision, my rite of passage to manhood, a ritual of rebirth that transformed me from a mother-reared boy into an accepted male member of our village community. For two weeks prior to the ordeal, I had been forcefully separated from my family and secluded in a small red-mud hut palisaded deep in the village shrine, together with three other boys who were to share the same honour with me. The witchdoctor and shrine guardians shaved our heads, removed all our clothing, smeared our bodies with sacred white chalk and forced us to scavenge the bushes for our own meals or starve. They also tutored us on the lore of our people, secrets and taboos of our clan and the conduct and responsibilities that a true son of the clan must always display. Finally, they made us attack each other in brutal fights designed to build our endurance, ensuring that when the sharp blade of the witchdoctor's knife sliced off our foreskin, we would take the pain like the real men we would become, without a whimper, tear, or groan. It was our duty to bring honour to our families and our ancestors by entering the passage of manhood like true men, brave and fearless.

I fulfilled my duty with honour, bringing pride to my watching father and kinsmen, who clasped my arm in camaraderie and gave me endless gourds of palm-wine to drink, a man's drink for a newly-made man. Despite the medicinal herbs coating my exposed organ, the blood continued to drip down my thighs, leaving a sticky warmth that was slightly repulsive to me, even as it reaffirmed my pride and the honour I had brought my clan. My father carried my bloodied foreskin in the special leaves that would ensure its male spirit returned for a rebirth into the clan. As I was the only son between two daughters, it was vital that more males be born into our family to ensure the perpetuity of the clan.

Mama was in tears when I returned to our house later that evening and was promptly transferred to Papa's room to recover, instead of wallowing in her soft and gentle care as had been the norm in my boyhood days. Papa's room was a new and strange experience for me, as it was a room my feet had never entered until the day I became a man. Even Mama was barred from the sparse room with its permanently shut wooden windows, which blocked the sunlight and cloaked the room in perpetual gloom. She left my food outside Papa's door while calling out loving greeting to me through the gap at the bottom of the door.

I stayed silent to Mama's questions, refused to speak to her despite my desperate yearning to share my pain with her and feel her loving arms around me, as in my childhood days. But tradition now dictated that as a man, I treated the womenfolk in my household like the children they were and addressed them only when it was necessary and unavoidable. How I wish now that I had ignored tradition, that I had bolted out of Papa's dark and dreary room to embrace Mama as my heart craved. For on the third day following my circumcision ritual, the same day that I found Papa's two grey men, Mama died.

III

I discovered the two grey men before I learnt of Mama's death. The sudden and loud clatter underneath Papa's bed, followed by a violent shuddering of the bed, had me leaping from it like one stung by a scorpion. My heart pounded like a woman confronted by a snake in her kitchen. Despite my lingering pain, I forced myself to my knees as I peered into the dark space underneath Papa's bed, expecting to see several big rats scurrying across the room. Such was the ruckus going on under that bed.

What I saw, instead, was a sight that brought a loud gasp to my lips, even as my eyes widened with shock and awe. In the dark gloom beneath Papa's bed, two squat men glowed with blinding brilliance, two identical wooden men, each the height of my school ruler, twelve inches tall, one with eyes that glowed a bottle green and the other, a pair of blood-red orbs. The men were short, resembling sturdy dwarves of the greyest skin. They were garbed in leather loincloths, their faces knife-scarred with a criss-cross of thin, red lines. Thick, blubbery lips leered malevolent smiles that held evil secrets from ancient, unknown realms. Where their hair should have been, endless gnarled fingers clawed the empty air, as if seeking a soft throat to strangle. By my reckoning, there must have been at least, twenty pairs of small, wriggling hands on each statue's head.

The grey men were on their feet, dancing a macabre dance, their hands linked as they hopped as high as the bed springs would allow. The bed shook violently each time they bumped against it, as if powerful fists pummelled it. They kicked their legs wide, executed a furious twirl, fell flat on their backs before leaping up again to perform the same maniacal dance. Each time their bodies hit the cement flooring of Papa's bedroom, they made a loud clatter that sounded like broken crockery and wild clapping. It was that strange sound that had dragged me from Papa's bed to my crouching position on the floor.

At first, I thought Papa had bought some secret battery-operated gift for me as a reward for my bravery during my initiation rite, albeit, a terrifying gift. I reached my arm further to grab hold of the dancing men.

They bit my hand. The two dancing men bit my hand, hard and long, till I thought I would die from the pain. An agonized howl escaped my lips as I stared with shock-widened eyes at the bleeding imprints of two sets of tiny teeth on my hand. The wound burnt, as if someone had poured petrol on my hand and set it on fire. The pain was like nothing I had ever experienced, worse than the slice of the witchdoctor's knife. My scream was long and loud.

Before my howl died out, I heard a louder shriek from beyond Papa's shut bedroom door, a female shriek, my big sister's voice. Dembeh was five years older than me and was already betrothed to the son of Papa's friend. She carried herself with the decorum of a respectable woman, her walk as gentle as her voice. To hear her scream shocked me out of my pain and sent me stumbling out of the room. As a newly-made man, it was my duty to protect the women in the household in Papa's absence.

"Mama is de...dead," Dembeh stuttered, tears rolling down her cheeks as she hiccupped deep gulps of air. "Our mother... our mother...she's dead...dead...."

I stared at my sister, unable to speak, unable to comprehend the impossible. *Mama was immortal—permanent. Mama had spoken through Papa's shut door to me only that afternoon when she brought me my lunch. Her voice had been as gentle and loving as ever, the strong and cheerful voice of life and longevity. How could she be dead? How could she cease to live, so suddenly, without warning?* I must have voiced out my confused thoughts because Dembeh's voice pierced through my stupor.

"She said she was seeing smoke, that her sight was vanishing even as she spoke to me," Dembeh cried, beating her chest repeatedly with her clenched fist, her bewildered eyes red and swollen. "I went to get water for her to wash her face, just in case she had accidentally rubbed peppery fingers on her eyes. When I returned, she was stretched out on the floor where you now see her, her legs kicking. It was as if her arms fought an invisible foe. She was fighting blindly, her sight gone, just the whites showing. She shrieked at them, the invisible demons, even as she prayed the Hail Mary. I tried to help her, but she kept punching me when she punched the empty air. I saw nothing; I swear there was nobody else in the room, just Mama, thrashing on the floor. Then, she screamed Papa's name, over and over. She screamed Papa's name and cursed him repeatedly before she started choking. Jesus help me, I saw her neck compress inwards as she choked and fought. I tried to pull her away, remove her from the demon attacking her. But it was as if her body was filled with the entire *Asattah* River—that was how heavy she became. Twenty men could not have lifted her from that floor. She went still, and I tried to wake her. That was when I saw the hands, the grey hand-imprints on her neck," Dembeh shuddered, staring at Mama's prone body with stunned eyes that mirrored the state of my heart.

I stared at my mother's corpse, stared at her face, her terror-whitened eyes that sent great chills down my spine. Whatever it was that she'd seen before death stole her life must have been truly terrible. The ghastly death grin on her face reminded me of the black masks of the terrifying *Mgboko* masquerade of my tribe, the three-headed incarnate of the death-deity that stole unwary souls. The unnatural stillness of her splayed limbs sent such terror to my soul, I thought my breathing would cease. But, what brought the greatest horror to my heart was the sight of Mama's neck. For, stamped on the dark skin of her neck, were the clear imprints of several pairs of grey hands, skeletal claws that marked her with death!

"She was cursing Papa...cursing him as she fought death," Dembeh said, her voice low, pain-filled. "Why would she curse Papa? What are those hand-marks on her neck? Whose hands are they? How could something squeeze the life from her throat without being seen? It can't be an *Amosuuh*, night-flyer. They work their evil while one sleeps and dreams. It can't even be the *Nsudooh*, Chest-Squatter, since that witch needs you asleep before sitting heavy on your chest and squatting the life out of your heart. But Mama wasn't sleeping or resting. She was standing, talking to me as normal as the next person before the smoke stole her sight. By the time I returned with the water she was on the floor fighting for her life. What are we going to do? What's going to happen to us? Oh, Holy Mary, protect us from evil."

Dembeh did several rapid signs of the Cross, which I quickly imitated. They were looking to me for answers, my big sister Dembeh, and my little sister, Namazziah. After all, I was now the man in the family in Papa's absence. But I didn't feel like a man, didn't want to be a man, anymore. I wished I were a girl—that I could cry the same free tears they shed for Mama without shame. All I wanted was for Mama to open her eyes, her warm and loving eyes that had been the cocoon of my life. Then, I would tell her I was sorry for not talking to her through Papa's locked door, that I hated being a newly-made man, that I was so sorry that I couldn't save her from the evil that stole her life. As my two sisters looked to me for answer, all I saw in their eyes was my failure.

IV

On the day Mama died, eleven young women collapsed in our village and died, each of them marked with the ghastly grey claw-marks around their necks. The village witchdoctor said the dead women, including Mama, were water sisters from a secret coven, the *Mamiwater* coven. He said they were the spawns of the evil river-goddess, *Mamiwater*, she of the forked tail, fish skin and human head, she who lured the souls of good men to their doom through her acolytes that wore the skin of human females.

For some unfathomable reason, *Mamiwater* had decided to call home her twelve evil daughters in one fell swoop. *For, how else could one explain the grey hands of death on all the dead women or the fact that they all died simultaneously on the same day, the same hour, and in the same gruesome manner?*

Mama, together with the eleven young women that died with her, were buried in vertical graves at the cursed forest without coffins, their eyes plucked out to ensure they would never find their way back to plague the families they left behind. Then, their corpses were pushed heads down into the vertical graves in an upside-down burial that would sink them deep into the supernatural sea and prevent them walking the earth again as the restless dead. The graves were filled with water to expedite their journey back to their evil realm before being sealed. Each of the cemented graves had sturdy wooden crosses embedded in them, to ensure the power of Christ held the soured souls down in the grave-soil for good. I did not believe that Mama was a *Mamiwater* daughter—that any evil tainted the devout Christian soul of my good mother, who spent as many hours on her knees praying to her Virgin Mary as she did caring for us. But, the witchdoctor had spoken, and the entire village believed.

Mama's death pushed away all thoughts of Papa's two grey men from my mind, especially as I stopped sleeping in his bedroom. The bite-marks eventually healed, although they left a permanent scar on my left hand, a scar which reminded me that what I'd witnessed underneath Papa's bed wasn't the wild imaginings of a confused mind. Within six months of Mama's burial, Papa moved us out of our small house in Mbaleyi village and into a large mansion in the big city of Kiraya.

Our new house was a sprawling mansion built in the style of the old colonial masters, a popular style amongst the rich and powerful in our country. Papa had become a big name in the government since Mama's death and important people came from all over the country to confer with him on vital political matters. The house we now lived in was a large story-building with six bedrooms, two reception rooms and four bathrooms. It had high roofs and high glass windows with intricate and ornate designs on the plasterwork both inside and outside the building. Rich oak panelling and thick red velvet drapes gave it a dark and foreboding air even on the sunniest of days. Even without the air-conditioning installed to keep the house cool as it roasted underneath our tropical sun, it still managed to remain chilly on most days, a cavern of stalagmites and stalactites.

Amongst the various artwork dotted around the mansion, were a pair of midget grey men in loincloths and knife-scar-ified faces, sculpted in fine Plaster of Paris and moulded into the two massive columns adorning the entrance of the house. The same twin figures were affixed on Papa's bedroom door as white-painted wood carvings. Seeing their gnarled finger-hair and leering faces always left me with a feeling of unease and re-vulsion, even fear at times. It brought back unwanted thoughts, made me gaze intently at the shadowy teeth-marks on my left hand. With everything that had happened, I figured it was best not to mention to Papa that I had discovered them dancing un-derneath his bed on the day Mama died. I did not want to incur his ire.

Occasionally, I would think about them, wondering again if they were electrically operated, something that might ease my mind about the bites I'd received when I touched them on that fateful day of Mama's death. I would have liked to inspect them in the light of day, but Papa kept his bedroom door permanently locked and try as I did, I never got the chance to view the two grey men again until it was too late.

V

A year after Mama's death, Papa married a second wife, a younger woman called Nasicheh, who had very thin legs sup-porting her rounded hips. My uncles said that Nasicheh's broad hips were a good sign that she would bear strong sons with ease. Their only reservation about her was the fact that her beautiful gap-teeth were not natural but had been bequeathed by the vil-lage gap-maker, the woman to whom young women visited to acquire the beauty of a gapped smile. There was no guarantee that Nasicheh's children would inherit the highly-sought beauty of a gap-teeth from an artificially acquired set. With my big sister, Dembeh, now married and away at her husband's home, coupled with my prolonged stay at the exclusive boarding school I attended, my little sister, Namazziah, was left alone with Papa and his new wife.

Three years into their marriage, Namazziah informed me that our stepmother was finally pregnant. It was a long-awaited event and one which came as a relief to the entire family, as the clans-men were already talking about marrying another wife for Papa to bear him another son. A second piece of news on the same week came as a great shock to me, the news of my father's accident, a freaky accident that would have been fantastic to the ears had my two eyes not seen Papa after the misfortune. My sister, Namazziah, witnessed everything, together with several house-servants in Papa's employment. Briefly, this is the account of event as it was narrated to me by Namazziah.

On the day of the accident, as I heard it, Papa had walked out of the front door as was his norm, headed to his Mercedes Benz car parked within the large compound of his mansion. Suddenly, from nowhere, a volt of vultures descended on him and started attacking him. Witnesses said the birds exhibited signs of supernatural possession by malevolent spirits, such was the ferocity of their attack on Papa. Even as the house-servants chased the hulking birds with brooms and sticks, they contin-ued to peck at Papa, intent on plucking out his eyes, until he managed to escape into his car. And even then, the vultures would not give up their attack, flinging themselves against the car windows and windscreen till the driver drove away with Papa, headed to the city hospital.

Papa's face was almost as scarred as the wooden faces of his two grey men when I visited him at the hospital. The vultures had left so many deep wounds on his face that he looked like a pox-ravaged victim. But, what got people talking even more than the bizarre attack itself was the sounds the house-servants claimed they'd heard, emitting from the throats of the vultures. Everyone who witnessed the attack said that they'd heard the vultures shriek in a female voice as they attacked Papa, an angry voice that kept screeching the name, "Akelloh! Akelloh!" as they pecked at him with vicious tenacity. *Akelloh! Papa's name!* It was terrible enough that the vultures had attacked with such intelligent malevolence, but for vultures to speak in human tongues was unheard of.

Other tongues soon ran loose with wild theories, stories that ran from the fantastic to the absurd. They opined that the vultures were birds of death, corpse-eaters whose presence signified evil; therefore, Papa must have offended a powerful enemy, likely a spurned mistress who was out to hex him with powerful juju or a jealous political foe. Whatever the truth of the matter was, Papa immediately put his men to work, sculpting and embedding several more statues of his two grey men around the house till our house resembled a temple to his wooden dwarves.

In time, things returned to normal once again in our household, till the next accident occurred, this time an unexpected and vicious attack by the faithful family dog, Brutus, a gentle mongrel we had owned from the time we first moved into the town mansion. Namazziah told me that just like the vultures, the dog went suddenly crazy, barking in a chilling female voice which shrilled Papa's name as it attacked him, goring his legs as if they were raw carcass. Brutus was put down and again, tongues wagged about Papa's enemies and supernatural hexes.

By the time a swarm of bees arrived on a cool Harmattan morning and overwhelmed Papa with enough poison to put him in hospital for several days, the rumour mill concluded that a curse had been placed on him by an *Iweh*, a Grudge Spirit, a terrifying curse executed by animals, birds, insects, and even parasites. *Iweh* was known to use every living creature of nature to attack the cursed. Again, Namazziah swore that the bees had called out Papa's name in the familiar screeching female voice. I laughed at Namazziah's words, scorned her superstitious drivel, even as I marvelled over the frequency of the strange attacks on Papa.

Now, I wish I had paid more attention to the rumours, that I had not dismissed my little sister's words with the arrogance of adolescence, which at the time was my swaggering companion, until the awful events in England unfolded before my unprepared eyes. Even now, I wonder if it's too late for me, if the cold autumn nights of this strange and desolate land will yet be my doom.

VI

After the attack of the bees, there were no further incidents in our house until the day my stepmother went into labour. The event coincided with Papa's final accident. It was also the day I heard the chilling clatter of broken crockery and wild clapping coming from Papa's locked bedroom, a terrible sound I recalled from a long-suppressed memory of something inexplicable that occurred on that accursed day of my mother's death.

I recall there had been an air of excitement that day after Nasicheh was rushed to the hospital early that morning to deliver her baby, a baby everyone hoped would be the long-awaited male child to bolster Papa's bloodline. My withered foreskin, salvaged from my initiation rite, had been mashed into a paste for Nasicheh to eat earlier in the day, ensuring she would deliver a son back into the clan. Papa had gone along with her to the hospital while Namazziah and I stayed home to await the news.

I can't recall what it was that took me upstairs sometime around noon, except now I wish I'd never climbed those tiled stairs to walk the long corridor that took me past Papa's locked door. I wish I'd been born deaf, bereft of hearing, then perhaps I would have been spared the terror of those ghastly, clacking sounds coming from Papa's locked door.

I froze where I stood outside Papa's door, the spot where my sister and I used to await his exit from his bedroom every morning to recite the obligatory, "Good morning, Papa. God bless you, sir." We would follow him downstairs, walking sedately behind him as he led us into the dining room, where Nasicheh waited with our breakfast. Except now, I didn't want to wait, didn't want to do a sedate walk down the stairs, didn't want to hear the horrible clamour going on behind the locked door of Papa's bedroom. I wanted to bolt down the stairs and keep running till the sounds disappeared. The clamour was like nothing I'd ever heard, the din tenfold multiplied to the one I'd heard on the day Mama died.

But I wasn't a child now, a boy nursing a mutilated genital and an unhatched bravery. I was almost eighteen years, a young man about to embark on a university program. I took several steps, slow steps on weakened legs, towards Papa's door. I reached out an arm and turned the knob. The door opened. *The door opened!* Papa's bedroom door that was always locked, opened easily and widely, as if someone—*something*—wanted me inside. The clamour was now so deafening I wondered why Namazziah and the house-servants weren't running up the stairs to investigate, why I was the only one standing with my heart in my mouth, desperately willing my man-heart to prove its bravery.

I entered the bedroom, the familiar dreary gloom of Papa's old bedroom in our village house where I'd first encountered the two grey men. As I expected, the din was coming from underneath Papa's bed, a bed identical to the one he had in his old house, a bed so at odds with the opulence of the mansion that it may as well have belonged to a pauper. It was as if Papa had lifted his old village bedroom and planted it in his opulent city mansion. The bedroom size was the same, smaller than every other bedroom in the mansion. Even the en-suite bathroom I spied across the bedroom, was twice the size of the tiny room. It stunned and baffled me to discover that Papa, wealthy and powerful Papa, who lived in this magnificent colonial-style mansion, slept in a room which would have shamed a beggar. A bad feeling of déjà vu crawled over my body as I stooped to look under the bed, the same bed with its wire-mesh springs that I knew—*just knew*—would squeak if I sat on it.

They were underneath the bed, the two squat wooden men with their burning red and green eyes and hair of wiggling fingers. Everything about them was the same as the first time I saw them, except their positions. The green-eyed dwarf was lying on the floor as if asleep, yet, his green eyes were wide open, staring straight at me with that terrible leer that sent terror-thuds to my heart. The red-eyed grey man was the one making all the clamour. He was doing a wild solo dance, hopping and banging himself against the bed and the floor with maniacal frenzy. His eyes glowed so brightly they lit up the gloomy room with a dim, red hue.

Suddenly, it turned and fixed its blazing gaze at me. Something evil, ancient, spewed from its lips in a thick, sulphuric smoke that quickly fogged up Papa's room. A sudden chill coated my skin in goosepimples. I stumbled away from the bed and ran out of the room, my heart pounding and my breath coming out in hot gasps. Even before Papa's car drove into the compound and delivered the news that Nasicheh, my young and beautiful stepmother, had died in childbirth with her stillborn daughter, I knew—*knew*—that Papa's two grey men had an evil hand in her sudden death.

By the end of that terrible day, we would all hear in the news that twelve young women had died at the town's hospital, each of them while birthing stillborn babies, each, eerily marked with what seemed like imprints of grey-white fingers around their necks. The news commentary pondered on the phenomenon being a new kind of disease similar to Ebola, Lassa Fever or Marburg virus. But I knew the terrible truth, the evil secret that lay underneath my father's bed, two malevolent entities that I now knew fed on the innocent blood of young women. Suddenly, my heart iced in fear for the lives of my big sister, Dembeh, and my beloved little sister, Namazziah.

VII

Papa was struck by lightning on the day that my stepmother died. Or rather, his mobile phone was struck by lightning as he spoke to a friend, leaving his face a charred mass of blistered flesh. If ever proof was needed of his guilt in his wife's death, this was it. Even as he fought for his life at the hospital, people were already saying that his sudden ascent to wealth just after the inexplicable death of his first wife, smacked of something supernatural, wicked. The death of his second wife in a similar manner, a young woman of broad hips, who should have delivered her baby with ease, pointed to his mischief, something now confirmed by the lightning strike. *For, who didn't know that lightning only ever struck the wicked and the guilty?*

Several weeks after the lightning strike, Papa left the hospital with a face that brought nightmares to both children and adults. He returned to the house a recluse, permanently confined to his bedroom. He instructed that no visitors be received save for our village witchdoctor, the same man that had performed my circumcision all those years ago. The witchdoctor arrived as soon as Papa was discharged from the hospital and moved into Papa's bedroom with him. I had no idea what they did in that room all day and night. Several times as I walked past Papa's room, I would hear low voices and strange gurgles, as if someone was drowning in a thick sludge of blood.

One day, several weeks after Papa's return, I received a call from him on my mobile phone while I watched the television in our living room. That was how we had been communicating since his return from the hospital. Papa informed me that he would be travelling to England to seek plastic surgery for his facial burns. I was to travel with him to England. The news gave me a thrill of excitement, as I'd always wanted to visit England. It was with joy that I packed my suitcase for our trip.

I saw Papa for the first time since his return from hospital on the day we travelled to London. The man that exited his bedroom that day, clinging to the witchdoctor, was a frail old man who appeared to be more bones than flesh. It was as if the lightning strike—which ruined his face had sucked the flesh and vitality from his body. His head was swaddled in white bandage that made it resemble a dinosaur egg. The black hat that covered his lightning-balded head, together with the dark sunglasses hiding his eyes, made him appear like a ghoul from a horror film. He leaned heavily on me as we walked through the immigration finger-printing process and into our first-class cabin on the British Airways plane. To my shame, I felt myself recoil from him as one would from a viper. My reaction was not a result of his strange visage, which drew numerous curious eyes on us. Rather, it was because of the dark secrets I knew, the deep suspicions that harboured in my heart, an unfamiliar feeling of distrust and even loathing, which now tainted the fierce love I once had for my father.

Our plane landed at Heathrow on a cold and dull October morning, which quickly numbed my fingers despite the jumper I wore underneath my thick jacket. This was a cold like nothing I had ever experienced in our homeland. Papa said it was nothing compared to the winter chill that would soon cloak this country in freezing snow. His voice sounded guttural, like the voice of a beast. It was a new voice, which had followed Papa out of his long confinement, a strange voice I was still struggling to get accustomed to. From the airport, we took a taxi to our rented apartment at Great Portland Street, less than a mile from Harley Street where Papa had an appointment booked with the Consultant the next morning.

I must have been very tired from the long trip because I fell into a deep sleep on the living room sofa after sharing a meal of flame-grilled chicken with Papa. Sometime in the dead of the night, I awoke to the familiar ghastly clattering sound emitting from the room where Papa slept. For several seconds, I was disoriented, unsure of my surroundings or the noises I was hearing. Then, as it began to sink into my conscious mind, a cold chill crawled up my spine like icy fingers, sending my heart racing. *Papa's two grey monsters!* It took all my man-strength to enter Papa's room across the small living room of our apartment. But this time, there was something in me that wanted answers, a rational explanation to the questions that had dogged me for years. Jesus in His sweet heaven! How I wish now that I never stepped foot inside that gloomy room of evil, that I never saw the things nor heard the words that stole my sleep and my peace from that day to this cold October morning, as I traverse this deserted park in search of salvation, inhaling the sad scents of a dying season, just like my dying sanity.

I found Papa awake and naked in his bed, his head still swaddled in the familiar white bandage. An eerie light filled the room, a light that came from the blazing bodies of the two wooden statues in Papa's hands. *Papa's dancing grey men!* In the pale light, I saw a sight that brought a soft gasp to my lips. Upon my father's bony shoulders were the defined imprints of two grey hands, giant claws that crawled from his shoulders to his chest! The skeletal fingers pulsed and stretched, great white worms that squirmed and burrowed, seeking Papa's heart underneath his flesh. I froze by the open door, my breathing fast and hot. Papa ignored my presence, or perhaps, he failed to notice me, such was his concentration on the two dazzling men he clasped in his hands. Papa was speaking to them, his voice hushed, urgent, desperate.

"Didn't I offer you my first wife, the mother of my children, as a sacrifice when you demanded it, great *Ubaah*, mighty deity of wealth?" My father cried, raising the hand that held the green-eyed grey man, his voice a plaintive wail that sent chills down my spine. He raised the other hand that held the red-eyed statue and spoke to it in the same anguished cry. "*Owuuh,* great Lord of death, haven't I sacrificed my second wife to you in exchange for longevity and good health? Haven't I served you well, been a good guardian and servant to you? Why do you seek my life now? Why does my first wife continue to plague me, to torture me from the grave, giving me no rest? I thought you would bind her soul and keep me safe. Tell me what to do, great deities. Command me and I will do it."

That was when I heard their voices, saw them in their true bestial forms as they began to metamorphose—thick, sulphurous smoke spewing from their flaring nostrils and belching from their leering lips. The stench was terrible, the funk of oldness beyond human existence. Papa gasped as he dropped them on the laminate floor of the room, nursing his blistered palms. The two fiends began to stretch, expand, and swell to unbelievable rotundity till it seemed they would burst, drowning us in a river of blood. The knife-scars on their faces dripped blood, a thick sludge that crawled along their bloated bodies like red worms, worms that rapidly grew into swarms of wriggling green-eyed snakes, hissing, crawling, filling my head with unspeakable horror. The claws that were their hair wiggled wildly, stretching into medusa-like manes. Forked tails replaced the legs that used to kick so gleefully into the air, tails that divided into themselves, birthing new swarms of wriggling snakes. Their heads slowly remoulded themselves into reptilian monstrosities with burning, slanted eyes and those blubbery, human-like lips, which none-theless failed to hide their sharp fangs.

Even as I stared in stunned disbelief, their skin shed their wooden hardness for the glittery sharpness of scales, shimmering like deadly creatures from the deepest rivers unknown to mankind and the ancestors. Or perhaps, even worse, ancient and putrid evils from the depths of accursed soils in unknown civilizations. When they spoke, their voices were the drowning gurgles I'd heard from my father's bedroom in our old home, Papa's new voice, voices from a dark place in a cold realm of pure terror.

"Your son! Give us your son, the blood of your blood, as our new guardian. Your time is done. You have served us well and have earned your right of entry into our paradise of eternal youth, waters of sweet wines and the soft pillows of a thousand women. A new custodian must be initiated, and a female of your bloodline must seal the ascension of your son to our guardianship. Give us the blood and soul of your only son. Just as your father and his father before him served us as guardians, so must you deliver your son into our service tonight."

I gasped; no, I think I screamed, because they were all looking at me, all three of them, my father and his bestial companions, their different-coloured eyes sharing a common greed—a voracious hunger for my soul. I saw my father rise from his bed, saw the blazing, colossal reptilian fish-demon beings glide towards me, their hissing snakes spreading a wriggling red carpet across the room like slimy gunk. A thick fog began to blind my eyes and steal my breath.

I ran. I ran far from that place of great evil till the cold dawn chased away that night of terror. I have been running for three days now, always glancing behind, feeling their malevolent pull on me, the renewed burning of the bite on my left hand, which has now started to bleed for the first time in almost six years. I have not slept in three nights because I sense them lurking at the edges of my sleep, smell their sulphuric funk in my cheap bed and breakfast room as they wait and watch for a chink in my guard. As I walk in this deserted park, inhaling the crisp autumnal air of damp foliage and earthy freshness, I wonder how

I can get through another night of sleeplessness. I wonder if this damp and cold country may yet be my eternal doom.

VIII

Last night, I had a dream. I'm not sure I can call it a dream since I have not slept for three nights and the vision came while I was in a foggy place between the realms of sleep and reality. In that near-fugue state of mind, I heard Mama's sweet voice as she spoke a message into my head.

"My son, go to The Old Chained Oak Tree, on the sacred grounds where the souls of loving parents have long protected their children and kept their innocent souls from the greedy grasp of death. I will await you underneath its withered boughs, by the strong shield of its great trunk whose twisting roots project through its ancient soil, within the safety of its sacred chains," Mama said, her voice, loving, strong. "There, we will await your father and his pale companions. Under the safety of its chained branches shall I fight death for the soul of my son. Beneath the rusty chains of the great Oak Tree shall we confront death and defeat it. Fear not, my son. We will fight them with the pure love of your mother and the holy love of our Blessed Mother, Mary. For what power can be stronger than the pure love of a good parent for their child? Go now; delay not. Your loving mother awaits you at the sacred Oak."

And so, I go, my hands empty save for the small Saint James Bible and mobile phone I clutch close to my chest. Inside the inner pocket of my jacket, my train ticket from London Waterloo to Alton station nestles against my pounding heart. I have researched the Internet for a tree in England with branches chained together. With all the miracles of modern technology I've witnessed since I stepped off the plane five days ago, I am certain that I'll not come across any such pagan relic as described by Mama in my dream. Yet, to my shock and joy, I have found the tree, just as Mama described, located at a town called Alton, in Shrewsbury. They say a great lord chained the branches to save his children from untimely death after a witch placed a curse on his bloodline, a chilling curse held back by the chains binding the great tree, a curse that states that for each branch of the Oak that falls, a member of his bloodline will die. I stare in wonder at the image of this mighty tree, its withered branches encircled with great rusty chains. It calls out to my heart, filling me with solace.

I pray I will get to my destination without event—that they will not interfere with my journey or find my soul within the crowded confines of the rushing train. I gaze out of the dust-coated window as we whiz past cosy villages, crowded towns and tired brick houses adorned with carved pumpkins which I hear the British call jack-o'-lanterns. I recall hearing some-where, perhaps on the BBC news, that today is Halloween, a national celebration where British children wear scary costumes and knock on doors asking for sweets. I've also read that it is the one night when the thin veil between the realms is temporarily ripped, allowing the departed entry into our world again.

From a distant place, a dark hole filled with buried memo-ries, my mind pulls out a strand of dazzling thought, a memory so incredible and bright it sets my heart pounding with hope. From my stress-suppressed memory, I recall that in my village of Mbaleyi, this day which the British people call Halloween, is also a special day to us.

Today is the Festival of *Owuuh*, the one night in a generation when the dead ancestors walk the earth again as skin-coated skeletons, for good or for evil. It is the night when wrongs are righted and potent messages revealed; when the thin veil be-tween the realms is temporarily ripped, allowing the departed entry into our world again, just like Halloween. That's what we were told during the preparations for our passage to manhood all those years ago in the shrine mud hut.

The elders swore that *Owuuh* is real, that they have seen our ancestors walk the earth the last time that great festival of the dead was held, years before my father's birth. I have no reason to doubt them, not when they are men of grey hair and wise eyes. It is on this incredible day of *Owuuh* that my mother has chosen to meet me underneath the fettered boughs of The Old Chained Oak Tree.

I smile, and my smile is broad, just like the great trees I see beyond my window as the train rumbles past, trees whose multi-coloured leaves are a riotous collage of extreme beauty, on this bright autumn day that has suddenly become the most beautiful day of all.

My heart races to the fast beat of the train, a race of joy, a lifting of darkness. For now, I know with unwavering faith that all will be well.

GOD'S COUNTRY

Christa Miller

Maia stood on the curb and gazed across the intersection at the wide flat fields, left plowed under and barren for as long as she could remember. In just a few short weeks, come the spring thaw, her father would tear it all down, plow the fields under, and start to construct the new microprocessor plant he'd been planning. Reclaim the land, give it positive meaning, a fresh start, a new legacy. Something that was desperately overdue for this town.

The tears that had tracked down her cheeks had long since dried, but their salty traces remained, tightening the skin where they had fallen. A smattering of raindrops showered around her, and Maia lifted her face to them, let them wash away the salt and with it, the pain of the weekly argument with her Sunday school teacher. She scrubbed at her skin with the sleeves of her sweater, then carefully stepped off the curb onto the empty, quiet roadway. She began to cross.

She would never fit in. That much was clear. No matter how hard she tried to keep an open mind to what Mrs. Waggoner or any of the others said, something always tweaked her the wrong way. She could never seem to stop herself from speaking up, and neither Mrs. Waggoner nor her classmates could ever seem to stop themselves from shutting her down.

It was the same sort of thing, she knew, that had driven her classmate Phillip Lamb to stand up last fall during Pastor Kraft's sermon and publicly declare his atheism. Perhaps that was why she was out here now, following in what were purported to be

Phillip's last steps, alone out here among the broken corn stalks and frozen earth. Where outcasts deserved to be.

Still, Phillip had come out here before her father had purchased this land. If anything, Maia felt, her desire to follow his footsteps—to walk the same land, explore every shadowy corner away from prying eyes and grabbing hands—was disingenuous. How much of an outcast could you be when your father owned the land you cast yourself out to? No, Maia couldn't say she had anything in common with Phillip Lamb. She couldn't even emulate his rebellious streak the right way.

She made it to the other side, stepped carefully onto the dry, ice-crystallized dirt. The crunch of it seemed unnaturally loud in the silence, and she had the sudden irrational thought that she would awaken something beneath the ground, some long-dormant creature that would reach up from beneath the topsoil to grasp her by the ankles and drag her down, down, down.

Just like it did to Phillip.

Nonsense. No creature lived under this land, any more than one lived under her bed at night. It simply wasn't possible, not on a brilliant morning like this. The earthy smells and fresh air and sun weren't quite as invigorating as a good storm, but they enlivened her in a way she never felt in church or at home, closed in by four walls and people's expectations. She stood for a few moments, breathing deeply. Then she took another step onto the field.

Because it wasn't as if Phillip had actually died here. He'd simply disappeared. The farmland was a convenient scapegoat, especially when the days mounted with police finding no trace of the teen. Some said that Phillip had spent his final hours either daring or making good on a bet with his friends. Others said he had, under the weight of his own shame for embarrassing his family, skipped town entirely, hitched a ride with a trucker or a circus. A few whispered that his disappearance was to be expected, happening as it had on cursed land.

What would people say about her when she disappeared? Maia guessed it would depend on who was talking. Her teachers and the church ladies like Mrs. Waggoner would cluck their tongues, say it was no surprise such a willful and disobedient child had gotten herself into a pickle. Her peers probably wouldn't even notice, the same way you walked on in comfort after getting rid of the rock in your shoe. And her father...well, her father would be sad, but he'd go forward with construction. He would build her legacy into this so-called cursed soil.

She moved across the field. The raindrops had stopped. The sky had brightened, and her confidence grew. Perhaps she could come here to live, hermit-like, in the structures that sat silent and shrouded in nearly perpetual mist in a hollow at the edge of the forest at the field's farthest edge. Perhaps those structures would reveal that Phillip had had the same idea. Even if he didn't come back with her, if she could prove he was still alive, she might even be a hero. The townspeople would have to respect her.

But they'd still never accept her.

Another strong wind kicked up. It was unexpectedly hot, suffused with the scent of burning—sweet wood smoke blended with something much more acrid, like some toxin. It surrounded Maia, cloying. The farmhouse, which should have been more visible from where she stood, was shrouded in darkness instead of its usual mist, as if the cloud had spawned a black fog to conceal the house and whatever grew there. Instead of raindrops, bits of ash drifted around her shoulders. The sky turned an ugly, dull grey-red.

Maia choked on a cry that had risen up her throat. Neither the news nor school had mentioned anything about wildfires, much less anything that could possibly burn out of control this quickly. Yet here she was, caught out in the middle of something gone horribly wrong. Even the ground felt wrong—spongy under her feet. She looked down. The corn stalks had softened, rotted in the mud. They curled around her feet and ankles, and she realized they weren't stalks at all, but tentacles, small ones—as if someone had planted baby octopi or jellyfish in the soil.

Now the cry she'd kept down threatened to rise into a full-fledged scream. She backed up, back towards the road, away from this hellscape, assuming she wasn't stuck here forever—

"Miz Maia! Where you going?"

With that, the farmhouse and the black fog and the cloud all disappeared, and Maia again stood at the cusp of the field on the corner. She turned slowly, just in case she was about to confront that blackness in humanoid form.

At the edge of the road idled a beat-up old pickup truck. The weathered, ruddy face peering out at her from the cab felt simultaneously like a lifeline and an entangling net. She should've known Mr. Gallagher would show up eventually, though she'd never heard him pull up. Her lifelong, self-appointed surrogate father, a close friend to her actual father. Had she been in the same mood as when she had first stepped off the curb on the other side of the street, Maia would have thought fast, come up with verbal parries to any reasons he might have posed to get her to come back into town with him. *I don't need a guardian*, she would have told him; *I need to be alone.* Yet the other world, with its bizarre colors and features caught up to her, made her knees weak and shaky. She found herself shifting her feet in case tentacles sprouted there, twitching her shoulders against anything that might reach across the field at her back. She said, faintly, "I'm just out for a walk."

"Oh? Is this where you're supposed to be?"

Maia choked off the crazy laugh that rose in her throat. "Where I'm supposed to be is the last place I want to be."

He regarded her silently. It was impossible to tell what he thought. Normally, his non-judgment and careful concern made for a welcome bulwark against the church ladies who scolded her for running about in the rain with the other kids, or against the other kids themselves, who teased her for her boyish clothing preferences. Today, his scrutiny added to her nerves. More raindrops had begun to fall, though—cold and heavy this time. And there was the memory of that otherworldly place she'd stepped into, where she might find herself once more if he granted her wish to be alone.

Was that where Phillip Lamb had ended up?

She practically charged at Mr. Gallagher's truck. Once settled into the passenger seat beside him, she sat silent and shaking.

He put the truck in gear, swung around and back out onto the road. At last he spoke, as mild-mannered as he ever had been. "You look a bit pale, Miz Maia."

"It's colder out than I expected." She spoke so softly, she wasn't sure he'd heard her.

"Is that all it is? If you don't mind my saying so, you look spooked more than anything else."

Maia forced a smile that she knew was too thin and too strained. "Now what could have spooked me in that field?"

He gazed at her for a long moment before turning his attention back to the road. "You tell me."

It was as if he knew what she'd seen out there. Maia couldn't keep up the facade. She turned her face to the side so that she could stare out at the passing trees and houses, normal against the backdrop of blue sky and green earth.

"Why don't we start over," he said, more gently. "What brought you all the way out here to begin with?"

Maia breathed out, as she knew the question and its tone were designed to help her do. "I walked. Church isn't but half a mile away."

"Very true," he mused. "But that isn't what I was asking. What was it made you walk all the way out here?"

"I just couldn't stand to be in church anymore, is all."

His brow furrowed faintly. "Why? What's wrong with church?"

Maia folded her arms. For all his non-judgment, she couldn't bring herself to tell him the truth. Everyone had their line that couldn't be crossed, and Mr. Gallagher was, after all, one of the townspeople no matter how far outside their periphery he existed.

So, no, a half-truth felt safer. "There's a new family they're all fawning over. 'How wonderful that you're raising your children in faith! So many parents don't nowadays!'" She drew another deep breath, found some momentum to continue. "And inside of a week they'll all be gossiping about the kind of food the mom buys or the way Little Timmy fell asleep during the sermon. Like a five-year-old should be enraptured by a grown man droning on and on, especially since all Pastor Kraft ever talks about are farming analogies, when no one in the congregation even has a farm. And when the mom walks by they'll stop and smile at her with those syrupy smiles and it might take her a few weeks, but she'll catch on eventually that she's the subject, and she'll try to find a way to make friends with one or two of them just to have someone stick up for her, but they'll never truly accept her and eventually she'll become one of them, too." Maia stopped, drew a deep breath. She'd gone too far in her rant.

But Mr. Gallagher was laughing, though his pursed lips and red face told her he was doing his best to suppress it.

"Besides," Maia mumbled then, "I told them I felt closest to God when I spend time in Nature." Because Nature didn't judge you. Nature encouraged you to feel like yourself, like when you walked alongside the river that ran just outside of town and felt as free and as loose as the rapids tumbling over the rocks.

"You said that? That can't have gone over well."

That was putting it mildly. Tears again pricked at Maia's eyelids, remembering Mrs. Waggoner's scowl as she'd informed Maia that church was meant to be a safe haven both literally and figuratively, that the pull to be away from it was nothing short of a demonic influence.

The thing was, maybe she was right. What else could have been behind that smoky, spongy farm field? If God had been present there, He wasn't a god Maia would want any part of.

She shook herself out of it. "What do you do on Sunday mornings, Mr. Gallagher?" she asked, although she'd long suspected she was seeing it right now: he spent them patrolling the perimeter of the town, or at least this side of the border, looking for spiritual scofflaws like her.

"It's the only time of the week I get to enjoy this land without anyone else around," he said. "So I enjoy it."

"But why not go enjoy land somewhere else? Hike or go boating up at the lake?"

"Who says I don't?"

Maia stared out the passenger side window at the field. "I just can't see what there is to enjoy here. It's so...barren."

"It only looks that way from here. When you spend time with it, you see the life teeming below the surface." His voice took on a cast she couldn't identify, one that made Maia think of the nascent tentacles that curled around her toes.

She shuddered, covered. "You almost sound like you don't approve of the new plant going in."

"No. Don't mind me. Progress is progress. You're right: this land hasn't been farm country in many years. I'm just old enough to remember that. We may be reaping something different now, but the land is still good for it."

He sounded like he'd stopped short of saying something else, some condition he'd been about to put on his final words. They had pulled up to the church, and still Maia wanted to know what it was, seeking, she realized, some kind of reassurance about that land. "You still don't sound sure," she said, then wanted to take the words back, afraid they had been too flippant.

Once more, though, rather than take her to task, he spoke, slowly, as if measuring out each word. "I don't hold with what people say about the land. That it's haunted, or cursed, or what have you. And I respect your father more than I can express. He's been a good friend." He looked at Maia then, right in the eye. "But I don't think he realizes what he's getting into."

He'd parked around the corner from the church. From beyond the walls, the final notes of the closing hymn swelled. "But I left during the sermon," Maia murmured. She had the troubling thought that her foray onto the nightmare-farm had somehow disrupted time itself.

"Pastor must've run long, then." Mr. Gallagher winked at her. "You can tell your father you were walking the grounds. Go on, now."

She opened the passenger door, scooted out onto the carefully maintained church lawn. As soon as she shut the door behind her, he was off. Probably didn't want to face the gossiping nellies any more than she did. She headed to the stand of willow trees whose low branches she used to like to climb when she was little. With any luck, she could hide out under their boughs for just a little while longer, to think.

Her foray into the other farmland put Maia on edge throughout the remainder of the morning. With each step, whether it was out from underneath the willows when she could no longer avoid the nellies, or to and from the bathroom at brunch, she found herself prepared to cross over into that other dimension.

By the afternoon, she could stand it no longer, and as a steady rain fell, she followed her father into his workshop the way she hadn't done for at least a few years. Since, she realized, he'd told her that she was adopted.

He noticed, too, though he didn't let on whether he recognized the significance of her picking up her old habit. "What's going on, Maia-ronymous?"

She cut right to the chase, unwilling to hedge and risk being put off. "Dad," she said, "Were there ever wildfires? Out at the old farm?"

Her father began very deliberately to set out his tools on his workbench. "The year before you were born," he said. "Why?"

"No reason. I just thought I remembered—or heard—something. About it." Maia mumbled the last few words.

"Can't imagine why. It was a long time ago. The town survived. It was a few tough years, but we managed all right." He peered at her then, the edges around his gaze sharp and hard. "That isn't where you went when you left church. Is it?"

Maia's cheeks flared hot. "I was where you found me. By the willow trees. Walking the grounds."

He regarded her with that flinty gaze just a few moments longer, as if measuring what else to say, how far to go. Finally, he refocused on the tools in front of him. "It's about time we built on that land, you know. Our town has gotten by since then, but it's time to grow."

"Don't." The word seemed to spring from Maia's mouth of its own accord. Then more words surged up and out. "Don't build there, Dad. There's something wrong with that land. Something bad, poisonous. Building there will kill the town, not grow it."

Her father suddenly looked very old, caved in as if the lines on his face ran deep underneath, undermined the connective tissue. His hands shook. He placed them palms down on the workbench. "You were out there," he said. "Weren't you?"

"No, Dad. I promise." The lie rolled as easily off her tongue as her warning. "I was going to. But Mr. Gallagher found me and stopped me. I—I dreamed about it, is all. More of a nightmare. It must've really spooked me, I—" She stopped. Restarted. "Do you think Mr. Gallagher could tell me more about the fires?"

At that, her father faced her.

"Please don't bring it up with him, honey," he said. "That was the year he lost his wife. I'm sure he doesn't want to relive it."

"After fifteen years?" Mr. Gallagher, like her father, didn't seem the type of person to hold on to grief.

"Grief has a funny way of lingering." Her father picked up a tool, rubbed at it absently with a polishing cloth. Maia knew he was thinking of his own wife, gone nine years now, but what he said was, "Look at Mrs. Lamb since losing Phillip."

"But that's different. Phillip went missing. She doesn't know if she should mourn him or not."

"In any case. Please don't bring it up. Mr. Gallagher's already been through a lot." Her father paused as if weighing whether to continue. Finally, he nodded, just once, a decision. "I don't think you knew this, but he was a prime suspect in your schoolmate's disappearance last fall. The police spent hours interrogating him."

A stone dropped in Maia's gut. "But he never said anything about that."

"And he wouldn't. He doesn't like to dwell, as you've pointed out. That doesn't mean...events...can't still hurt him." The cords on the sides of her father's neck tightened.

She said, "But he knows just about everyone. He sees a lot, too. All the neighbor and business disputes he's mediated, the business owners like you that he's mentored. Couldn't that be why the police wanted to talk to him?"

"It could be," her father said, "but it wasn't."

He regarded her, then, in a way that was uncannily similar to Mr. Gallagher's gaze from that morning.

"People don't trust those who don't conform, but they don't realize sometimes those are the very people they need most."

It was as if the two men knew something about her that Maia herself had yet to learn. "So all those times you let him drive me home," Maia started.

Her father cut her off. "Stop right there. That man is the least of all the people you have to worry about. Can't you sense that about him?"

Maia stared at her feet. Of course she could. It was the reason seeing him down the corner from her bus stop made her feel safe, not stalked, and the reason she kept getting into his truck even when her peers whispered and snickered and outright told her he was creepy. No, he'd never given Maia that vibe. "Dad," she said then. "Did he have anything to do with my adoption?"

His mouth had a twist to it that made her think he regretted going down this path. "He found you. Abandoned on a roadside. He knew we couldn't have children of our own, and he suggested we be the ones to adopt you." He forced a smile. "I think that's enough for today, Maia-ronymous. Mr. Gallagher does a lot for this town. We should respect his privacy."

There it was. The thing everyone always said in this town when people wanted you to stop asking questions. People had started talking about Mrs. Lamb's privacy as soon as questions came up around whether Phillip had been out beyond the border, had flouted the town's notions around the order of things. The investigation had been fairly transparent up until that point. Maia suspected it had been closed altogether.

Her father turned back to his workbench. "I love you, sweetheart, but there are some things I'm not yet ready to talk about. Now, are you ready for the school week?"

Skipping school was easy. Easy to justify after the way her father had put her off, and easy to execute: her father dropped her off out front, she snuck right out the back. She'd seen Phillip and his friends do it, once, put two and two together from the way his friends struggled to keep a straight face while they asked for permission to leave homeroom or first period, then never showed up for the rest of the day. This morning, she bypassed homeroom altogether.

The school was slightly farther from the field than the church was, another quarter-mile or so, but flat and easy enough to walk. Normally, Maia would stick to the trail that ran between the neighborhoods, the better to avoid Mr. Gallagher. Today, she boldly walked the town sidewalks. It was risky—she might encounter some teacher or another student arriving at school late—but today she wanted Mr. Gallagher's reliability to work in her favor.

He took longer than expected to show. She could see the field up ahead by the time he passed her, on the other side of the road, headed in the same direction. She watched him heel the truck around in the middle of the empty road. He pulled to the curbside as he approached her. The passenger side window rolled down and then he was leaning across the seat to talk to her. "Shouldn't you be in school?" he called.

She stopped, leaned her arms on the door frame. "Yes," she said, "but I wanted to talk to you. No, it couldn't wait."

He sighed, faced the windshield momentarily. "Get in."

He would probably bring her back to school. *Best make it quick.* "You know how you asked me yesterday what spooked me in the old field?"

"Yes. You said you were cold."

"And that was true. But I was also scared. Mr. Gallagher, I saw something yesterday. I walked into this…I don't know what it was. It was the field, but like it had been on fire." The words came faster now, part of a jumbled rush that Maia couldn't stop. "And then my dad said there were wildfires the year I was born, but I shouldn't ask you about them, but I don't know who else to talk to because somehow I managed to *time travel?*" Finally, she stopped for a breath.

The truck slowed. They were coming up on a parking lot. Mr. Gallagher put his turn signal on. They parked on the far side of the lot, and he turned toward her. The way he looked at her sometimes, like now, made her feel both pretty and self-conscious, as if he knew a wonderful secret about her that she herself hadn't yet discovered. This time she saw something else: wonder—as if she'd exceeded his expectations and he couldn't decide whether to be impressed or intimidated. For the first time she wondered if her friends saw something in him that she didn't. She dropped her gaze to her lap, twisted her fingers.

He asked: "What did you see?"

"Never mind," she mumbled. "My father said I shouldn't bring it up to you."

"Why?" he asked. "Because my wife was lost?"

"Yeah." Maia glanced at him sidelong. "I'm sorry."

His face had softened. "She wasn't really my wife. Just a story I told the townspeople so reality wouldn't frighten them." He paused. "I'm still trying to decide how I'm going to explain you."

Maia turned towards him. "What are you talking about?"

The sky darkened. A few drops of rain spattered the windshield.

He didn't answer her directly. Instead, he said, so softly it was almost to himself, "You're so young. You weren't meant to find out until later. But maybe you're ready after all." He made no move to go anywhere, though, and was silent for so long that by the time he did put the truck back in gear, Maia had become convinced she was about to find out the things her friends had warned her about, that she was now certain Phillip Lamb knew.

He turned out of the parking lot, back in the direction of the farmland. Each time the truck slowed, for a stoplight or another vehicle, Maia considered opening the door, jumping out. But she stayed, and before long they were at the intersection that led to the field.

Mr. Gallagher said: "I'll take you home soon, Maia. But first, there's something I want to show you." Something in her face must have betrayed her fear, because his expression softened. "Don't worry. There are things you need to know about our town. And about yourself. It's nothing you won't be able to handle. But you do have a few choices to make. Basic growing-up stuff. Okay?"

No, not okay, Maia wanted to scream, but the light had turned green and they were moving on, across the intersection and onward between the wide, barren fields that stretched before them.

The road ended abruptly, just over a rise. It ran into, underneath, the soil as if the asphalt were an irritation that the field had simply grown over. Here was where Mr. Gallagher parked the truck, switching off the ignition. He motioned for her to get out.

She did, taking care to notice all the smallest details she could: the bright blue sky overhead, the rush of wind through the reeds that bordered between roadway and field, the hum of insects, the cry of gulls overhead. If she was going to die today, she wanted to go out in peace.

Still, if he wanted her to walk back into that field, she wasn't sure she could do it. The memory of yesterday's time travel, or whatever it had been, was too fresh, those tentacled beings caressing her feet as she stood by them. No pall of smoke hung over the farmhouse remains, yet she could not make herself walk across that roadway. Even the blue-black cloud that hung over the field several miles out, dark as the smoke from the scorched field, seemed to embody her dread. Thunder rumbled.

Mr. Gallagher came over to stand beside her, close, not quite touching. Instead of threat, though, Maia sensed the same familiar comfort she always had from him. Maybe he was an alien who had the ability to lull his human victims into a false sense of security. Well, so be it. She let her gaze follow his finger as he pointed out across the field opposite.

"You can see the farmhouse today," she said, doing her best to keep an even tone. "It's not covered in mist."

He nodded. "A hundred years ago, that farmhouse and that farm were built in much the same way and for much the same reasons as your father wants to build his factory. Thing is, the townspeople had no idea the land was already inhabited. At first, when cattle started to go missing, they blamed the tribe of Natives they'd pushed out to make room. But the cattle were never found, not even after the townspeople went in and slaughtered the entire tribe, and when the farmer's three daughters went missing, the Natives were blamed for that, too, even though there was no one left to kill.

"Over time, the narrative changed. It was said that the farmer who built that house had been up to unnatural acts with his daughters, and had killed them to cover it up. Eventually he died, and the farmhouse fell into ruin. But the thing beneath it remained.

"Three generations passed. The townspeople decided that the place was cursed, especially after people began to disappear from the land. Mostly kids, going out to the old farmhouse on a dare or to party. The adults knew better. Ultimately they caught on that there was more to that place than met the eye. They knew they needed a guardian. Somehow, they found a book at the library that held all the old rites, and they summoned me.

"And yet, a guardian can only go so far before his own energies are depleted. He's only temporary, you see, until a permanent solution can be found. The Natives the townspeople slaughtered could have told them that. In any case, I needed a way to focus my own energies. So I summoned an elemental, a fire spirit. I figured if she could scorch the earth, she could kill the thing in the ground.

"But I didn't nurture her. I summoned her, with all her power, but my mistake was thinking she came fully able to focus and direct her power. She died in the fire she conjured, and the thing lives on. Taking what walks onto its land." He gazed out across the field. "Like your friend, Phillip Lamb. I'm afraid it's growing—has grown—too big for me to guard any longer. Soon it'll be big enough to cross that boundary and take what it wants. Whenever it wants. Your father's plant…will just accelerate that process."

"The babies growing in the dirt," Maia murmured.

He glanced sharply down at her. "You saw them?"

"They grabbed at my feet when I went into the field. Why can't we see them from where we are here? Did I…time travel? Or walk into some other dimension?"

He stared off across the field. "No. You didn't."

He blew a long sigh from his nose. "What you saw was reality. I don't let the townspeople see it. It would scare them, drive them to…it would kill the town. So I keep it all shielded, hidden from view." He waved an arm.

To their right, down a slight incline, an old brick farmhouse had appeared. It sat at an angle to the road as if cold-shouldering visitors. It stood three stories tall, its shutters hung crooked, and holes of jagged glass gaped from the windowpanes. On the side, someone had painted a huge, blood-red skull, outlined in bone-white, two of the windows for eyes.

"This was my house." Mr. Gallagher gazed at it, his eyes pained. "I lived here until…until I had to hide it. I'm afraid I don't have the energy to maintain an entire shield, and also live behind it."

Maia backed up a few steps. Towards the road, and beyond that, the civilization she knew. "What do you mean, 'shield'?" She had to force the words out, and still her voice was small. "How was I able to see something you…hid?"

"That is the fifty million dollar question. You were able to cross the shield because you, yourself, are an elemental." His expression changed. He again regarded her with a mix of pride and fear. "You're more powerful than I ever imagined you could be."

"What are you saying? I've never even heard of—whatever you said, elements. Pastor Kraft would say they're demonic, and if he heard you talking right now, he'd say you are, too." Maia took another step backwards. "You didn't summon me. I'm just a person. That's all I've ever been. That's all I want to be. My own person."

"Yes, you are," said Mr. Gallagher. "But I did summon you. I've nurtured you. Well, with the help of your father. He raised you to know how to make your own choices, and you're almost mature enough now to make them. We can complete our work now that you know the full truth. But it has to be your choice."

Around them, the rain couldn't seem to decide whether to fall harder, or to stop. "My choice to do what, exactly?" Maia said slowly.

"Don't you see?" Mr. Gallagher gestured around them. "You summon storms with your moods. Always have." He pitched his voice lower, as if afraid the thing in the field could hear him. "You have to drown it. Use your power to bring down a storm that will kill it once and for all."

Maia clapped her hands to her mouth. The revulsion of it made her want to throw up. "So you summoned me, supposedly, so you could use me to kill something else, maybe get myself killed, too?" she choked out. "What gave you the right? My entire life, all anyone's told me is sit down, shut up, mind your own business, be a good girl. Now I'm supposed to rise up and find my power? Because the responsibility for saving you all rests with me? What am I, Buffy the Vampire Slayer? You can't have it both ways, Mr. Gallagher. I'm sorry." But she wasn't sorry, not really, in fact she was the least sorry possible, and the word was only a reflex drummed into her.

It must have shown on her face, because he faced her. Took both of her hands. "You're right. The town doesn't treat you like one of them," he said gently. In his voice, she heard edges she'd never heard before. "I thought that by giving you those sixteen years to come into your own, I was doing you a favor. More of one than I'd given Aine. So, sure. You could as easily choose to do nothing. Let the thing take over, take what it wants, including you and your power, if you wanted it to."

Maia yanked her hands away. Around them the rain fell more steadily. "What would happen then?"

"It would keep growing. Eventually it would reach the neighboring towns. Not like some sci-fi movie, but not the generations it's taken to spread here, either. If it feeds off you, it'll spread faster and farther."

"But it can be stopped now."

"Yes. It can."

"Say I do stop it. What happens after? Can't I just save everyone and go back to living my life?"

"No. Because you can control the weather. And you don't want to be around these people when that happens."

"But I'll be all alone."

"No. You won't."

Maia's belly flip-flopped. "Because I'll be with you? What does that mean? You and my dad, double-teaming me?" The rain fell as hard as ever. She had to shout for him to hear her, though she suspected she would've shouted anyway. "Did you hear what I said? I'm over people trying to control me, or make me control myself. Maybe I'll never be accepted, but at least let me live my life the way I want. Stop assuming I can't be responsible because I'm too young. Let me learn it for myself. And don't say the weather isn't something I can afford to make mistakes with. You can't have it both ways."

By the time she finished, the storm had become a swirling vortex of water and wind. It would be so easy to drown it all: the town, the beast under the field, the peers and adults who judged her, her whole life. That was what she'd been brought here for, wasn't it? To kill?

With a cry, she ran from Mr. Gallagher, scrambled up the slope toward the field beyond. Behind her, she heard him call out, but she couldn't hear what he said. She didn't stop. She reached the asphalt and kept running.

She didn't stop until she'd reached the middle of the field. Here it looked almost normal; Maia couldn't figure out whether this was the "real" world, or the shielded one. Her shadow had come faintly back into existence as the clouds overhead, spent, wafted apart to reveal blue sky underneath. She looked down. A small tentacle curled around her foot.

Maia stretched out her arms in front of her. They looked perfectly average, with their white skin and pink undertone and blue-green veins. They didn't weep water or anything, and if she raised them just so, the clouds overhead didn't respond in the slightest. Didn't gather when she brought her hands together, didn't scatter when she spread her hands wide.

Maybe that was what her friends had observed about Mr. Gallagher: it wasn't that he was a creeper. It was just that he believed some kind of delusion about her. It should be easy, then, to debunk the delusion for herself. Maybe snap some pictures.

A gust of cold wind kicked up. Maia shivered, then oriented herself. The farmhouse lay ahead and to her left. With a quick glance back over her shoulder—she half-expected Mr. Gallagher to have followed her, his ancient pickup kicking up clods of dirt and tentacle-cabbages—she set off.

The closer she got to the farmhouse, the warmer the air grew. A quarter-mile from the farmhouse a strong, hot wind unexpectedly pushed back. The sweet scent of burning wood mingled with the toxic chemical reek she recalled from the last time she had been in this place and time. It clung heavy in her nostrils as the ash fell all around her, the sky that angry grey-red.

Maia stopped for a moment to rebalance. The cloud overhead had reassembled. It now spanned the entire width of the farm fields, the blue-grey rings at its outer edges bordering a steely interior. It seemed to change shape as she watched, formed shelves of clouds, seemed to hollow out behind the shelves as if fashioned by an upside-down potter. It was fascinating, really: most storm clouds ended up partially concealed behind houses and trees. To watch it roll in from across an open field now seemed like a rare gift.

Maia continued on, careful to walk between the spongy tentacles that squished and curled underfoot. This time she focused on her destination—the farmhouse—once again shrouded in the inky black fog. She eyed the stormcloud above. Bits of cotton batting tore themselves off it, flew away like tumbleweeds in the dust. A few drops of rain fell on her face, enlivening her skin. More lightning flashed, bolts of stark white against the grey-blue clouds. The wind picked up the strands of her hair and flung them about her face and neck, as if the storm were a sentient being that liked to play.

Before long, though, the ground changed once more, became hardened and scorched. The corn stalks—tentacle stalks—lay charred and deadened across the ground, victims of the brush fire that had burned hot and bright on this land. The farmhouse had been caught, just like Mr. Gallagher said, and Maia noted that the black fog was really smoke, although like no smoke she had ever seen. It hung with well-defined edges over the farmhouse and the barnyard like a force field.

Which was, she saw on closer inspection, basically what it was. Around the house's perimeter something moved, undulated out from underneath the crevices in the foundation. More tentacles, except these were blackened, split open like overcooked sausages, weeping some kind of yellow liquid. As she watched, both fascinated and repulsed, the tentacles seemed to see her. They gathered together, elongating, stretching, reaching.

The farmhouse's front door crashed open. Maia stopped, paralyzed. Her heart hammered its way up into her throat. A figure stood in the doorway. It was human-shaped, but surrounded by tentacles that seemed to grow from its back. They, too, elongated in her direction.

But not before she saw the figure's face. Because it was Phillip Lamb staring back at her, his face twisted in agony. Whatever this thing was seemed to be absorbing him from the inside out. The only thing left, in fact, was his face.

Maia screamed, and the cloud above them burst.

The tentacles continued to reach through the torrent. Their suckers seemed to absorb the moisture before reaching farther towards her—seething with her storm-power contained within her. Mr. Gallagher had warned her, hadn't he? This thing would kill her and take her power, use it to grow farther and faster than he thought it would otherwise be able to.

She didn't want to die. Not today.

She spread her arms and called out in a language that wasn't a language, a tongue that came as naturally to her as walking and singing and even breathing. She ignored the way her voice quavered, focused instead on how the storm seemed to respond: to thrum with its own rhythm to the sound of her voice. It pushed both the stink and the heat from her, cooling her.

The figure in the doorway stumbled out onto the porch, waving its arm-tentacles, shouting some gibberish—which, for all she knew, was the same language she herself sang. The tentacles around the house's perimeter retracted, raised themselves up, drank in the water. Seemed to *grow*.

Around her, the vortex spun into a frenzy. Rain again spattered her face, but buckets of it poured onto the ground beyond. They made the Phillip-figure stop, turn the last of its face to the sky, to drink or to hasten drowning, Maia couldn't tell.

When it fell prone to the ground, all the tentacles began to retract, to withdraw from the teeming rain that battered their soft surface. Maia found herself standing in a puddle of muddy water that came up to her calves, and still the rain fell, because even if she wanted to, she couldn't stop. Even after the baby tentacles stopped reaching up from underneath their own puddles, even after they subsided and sank and flopped like dying fish at her feet, even though she knew on some level deep in her bones that it would deplete her, her rain kept coming. Like the deluge of criticism she'd received from the townsfolk, it made its way from her calves to her knees to her waist.

She couldn't control the floodwaters any more than she could control her storm-summons. As soon as she'd freed her feet from the mud, she lay back so that the water cradled her, the water surged toward the town. It rendered her as free and as loose as the rapids tumbling over the rocks, so that at last she felt like only herself.

BIOGRAPHIES

PATRICK BERRY is a writer and crossword constructor whose work has appeared in *Harper's, The New Yorker, The New York Times, The Wall Street Journal,* and numerous other publications. He lives in Athens, Georgia.

C.W. BLACKWELL was born and raised in Santa Cruz, California where he still lives today with his wife and two children. His passion is to blend poetic narratives with pulp dialogue to create strange and rhythmic genre fiction. He writes mostly crime fiction, dark fiction, and weird westerns. You can follow him on Facebook and Twitter.

MATTHEW BRADY is a young writer currently living in Nashville, Tennessee. He attended Belmont University in 2010, where he studied writing and literature before earning his bachelor's degree in 2014. He has had poetry and short fiction published in his college journal, and has self-published one novel titled *Aesop Street*. For more information on the author and upcoming works, visit www.lulu.com/spotlight/MatthewBrady.

MARK EDWARD BROOKS is originally from St. Louis, Missouri and now resides in San Marcos, Texas. He has two novels out, *Basement Things,* a horror novel and the short story collection *Through a Darker Eye.* He loves reading, writing and all outdoor activities and is looking forward to Halloween.

RUSSELL DORN is an author of horror and children's picture books. He is also co-creator of www.felipefemur.com, a free website for kids featuring games, stories, craft ideas, recipes, and more. Russell's adult horror stories have appeared in several publications and are due to appear in a handful of forthcoming anthologies. He is a graduate of the University of Nevada, Reno. Visit his website for more information: www.russelldorn.com Twitter: @DornRussell.

MARY FANCHER is an artist and writer living in Baldwinsville, New York with her husband and four cats. She possesses a degree in studio art from the State University of New York at Binghamton, and has displayed her art work in a number of galleries and juried exhibitions in New York, Oregon, Washington State, and South Carolina.

Her writing has included work in both historical fiction and horror. *John Lee,* a work of historical fiction, was one of the finalists for the 2014 South Carolina First Novel Award, and a finalist in the 2016 Faulkner-Wisdom Creative Writing Competition. Another historical fiction novel, *The Love Letter of John Henry Holliday,* was on the short list for the 2015 Historical Novel Society's Indie Editor's Choice Award. Her short stories have appeared in *The Horror Zine* and *Sanitarium Magazines,* while a short work of historical fiction will appear in the *Tahoma Literary Review's* fall edition.

ALI HABASHI graduated from the University of St. Andrews, Scotland with a degree in English and Management, and currently works in Boston at an academic publisher. When not at work she can usually be found drinking coffee and stressing about a self-inflicted creative project that in all likelihood has something to do with monsters or witches. Her short stories have appeared several times on *The Other Stories* horror podcast (Hawk and Cleaver) and this fall 2018 she will be featured in an anthology by Transmundane Press. Learn more about Ali Habashi's writing at alihabashi.com.

CHRISTA MILLER is too goody-two-shoes for the rebels and too rebellious for the good girls and boys—Christa Miller writes fiction which, like herself, doesn't quite fit in. A professional writer for 15+ years, Christa has written in a variety of genres ranging from crime fiction to horror to children's, but her favorite stories to write—and read—are those which blend genres. Two of her novellas have appeared in the *Running Wild Novella Anthology Vol. 1* and *Vol. 2 Pt. 1*. Her short stories have previously been published in the 2008 anthology *Northern Haunts,* in *Shroud Magazine, Out of the Gutter Magazine, Spinetingler Magazine,* and in a handful of online zines. Her affinity for the dark, psychological, and somewhat bizarre doesn't stop her from snuggling baby animals as a volunteer at a local wildlife rescue, adventuring with her two sons in rivers, swamps and salt marshes, or relaxing with a good book and a cold beverage in her hammock. Christa is based in Greenville, South Carolina.

NUZO ONOH is a British writer of African-Igbo heritage. Popularly known as, "The Queen of African Horror", Nuzo was born in Enugu, in the Eastern part of Nigeria (formerly, The Republic of Biafra). She first came to England as a teenager and attended The Mount School, York, (a Quaker boarding school) and St. Andrew's Tutorial College, Cambridge, from where she obtained her A-levels. She holds a Law Degree and a Masters Degree in Writing, both from The University of Warwick, Warwickshire.

Nuzo has been championing the alternative horror genre, African Horror, and has featured on multiple media platforms promoting this unique horror genre. She is the first African Horror writer to feature on *Starburst Magazine,* the world's longest-running magazine of cult entertainment. She has also made the front-cover of *Paranormal Underground Magazine.* Nuzo is included in the reference book, "80 Black Women in Horror" and her writing has also featured in multiple anthologies. She has written several blogs for *Female First Magazine* about African Horror and has been mentioned as one of the new voices in British horror writing making a positive impact on how black and minority races are portrayed in mainstream horror fiction.

Nuzo has also given talks at several events about African Horror, including the Warwick University Law Society.

A keen musician, Nuzo plays both the piano and guitar and enjoys writing songs when not haunting church graveyards and the beautiful Coventry War Memorial Park. Her book, *The Reluctant Dead* (2014), introduced modern African Horror into the mainstream Horror genre. Nuzo has two daughters and her cat, Tinkerbell. She lives in Coventry and is an active member of the Coventry Writers Group.

COPYRIGHTS

FINIS

NOSETOUCH PRESS™

Nosetouch Press is an independent book publisher
tandemly-based in Chicago and Pittsburgh.
We are dedicated to bringing some of today's most
energizing fiction to readers around the world.

Our commitment to classic book design in a digital
environment brings an innovative and authentic approach
to the traditions of literary excellence.

NEW & CLASSIC
Science Fiction
Fantasy
Horror
Mystery
Supernatural

The Nose Knows™
NOSETOUCHPRESS.COM

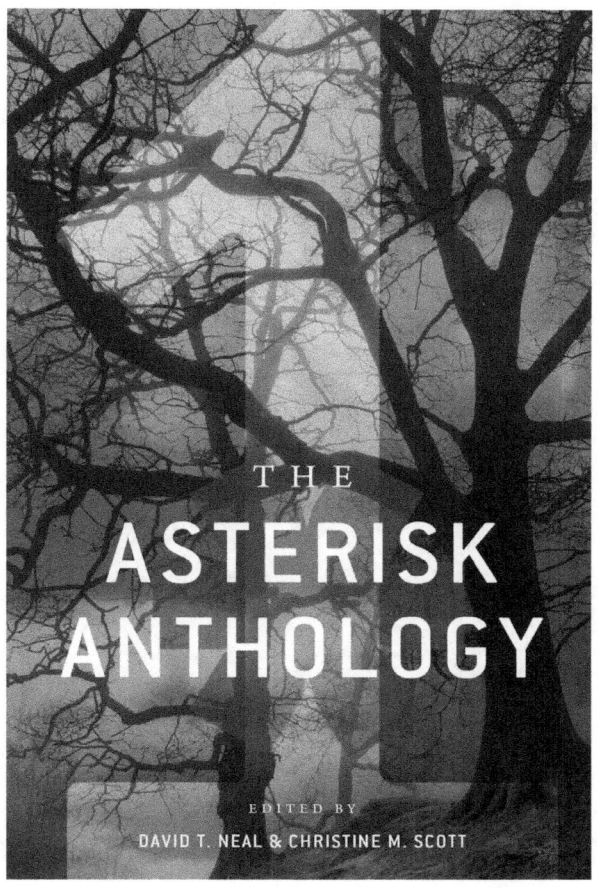

Covering four specific horror-related themes: Halloween, ghost stories, nautical terrors, and cosmic horror, The *Asterisk Anthology: Volume 1,* brings readers eight extraordinary tales from new authors of weird fiction, winners of the Nosetouch Press calls throughout 2017.

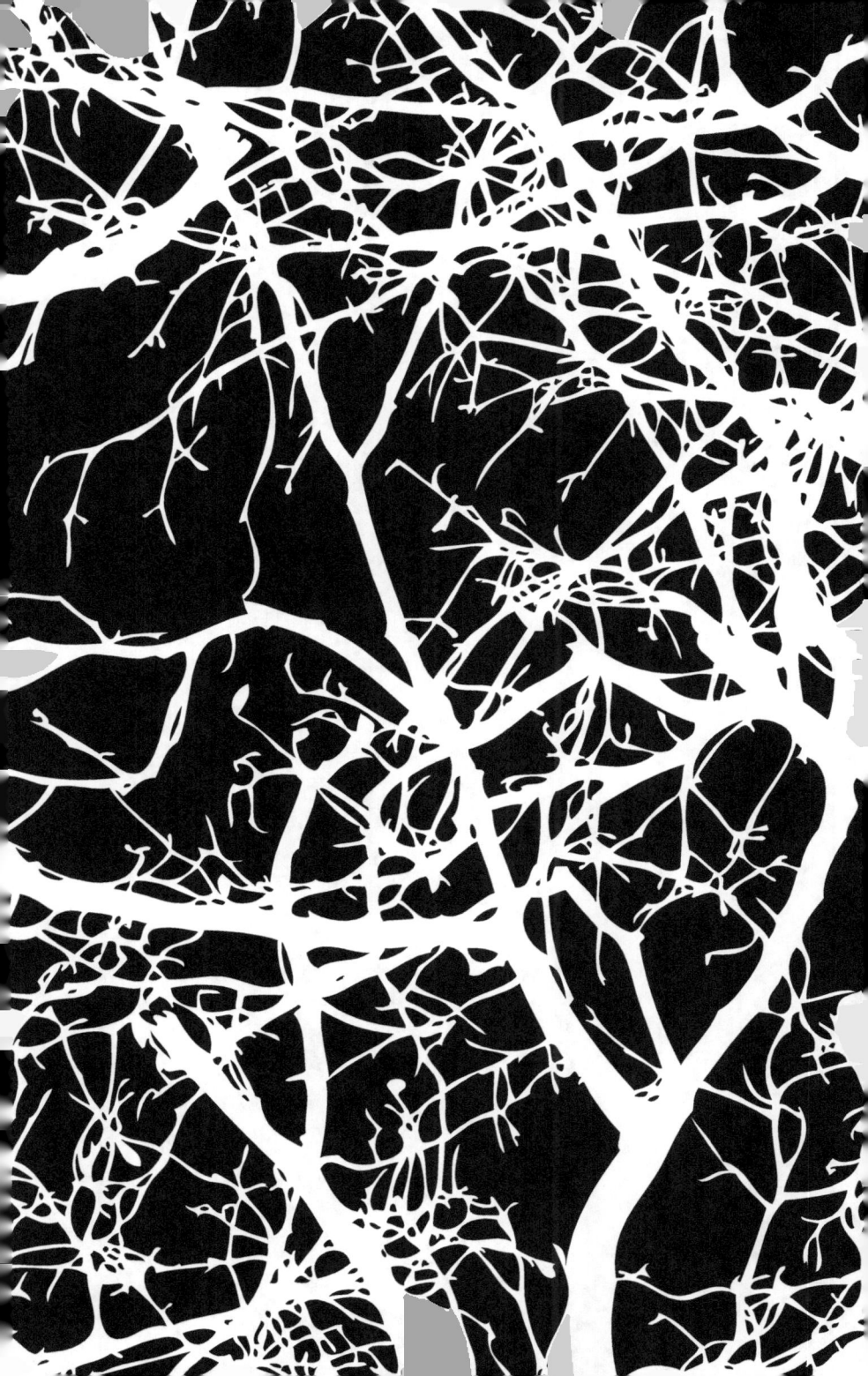